DAYS IN THE HISTORY OF SILENCE

Merethe Lindstrøm

TRANSLATED FROM THE NORWEGIAN BY Anne Bruce

DAYS IN THE HISTORY OF SILENCE

OTHER PRESS NEW YORK

Originally published as *Dager i stillhetens historie* in Oslo, Norway.

This translation has been published with the financial support of NORLA.

Production Editor: Yvonne E. Cárdenas

Text Designer: Chris Welch

This book was set in 11 pt Minion by Alpha Design & Composition of Pittsfield, NH.

10 9 8 7 6 5 4 3 2

Library of Congress Cataloging-in-Publication Data

Lindstrøm, Merethe, author.
[Dager i stillhetens historie. English]
Days in the history of silence / by Merethe Lindstrøm ; translated from the Norwegian by Anne Bruce.
pages cm
ISBN 978-1-59051-595-2 (pbk.) — ISBN 978-1-59051-597-6 (ebook)
1. Holocaust survivors—Fiction. 2. Norway—21st century—Fiction.
3. Domestic fiction. I. Bruce, Anne, 1952 April 22—translator. II. Title.
PT8951.22.I55D3413 2013
839.82'374—dc23

2012048598

Publisher's Note:
This is a work of fiction. Names, characters, places, and incidents either are the product of the author's imagination or are used fictitiously, and any resemblance to actual persons, living or dead, events, or locales is entirely coincidental.

I was the one who let him in.

Later I called him the intruder, but he did not break in. He rang the doorbell as anyone at all might have done, and I opened the door. It unsettles me still when I think about it. Really that could be what bothers me most. He rang the doorbell, and I opened the door.

So mundane.

Perhaps I had caught a glimpse of him that very morning at the bottom of the garden when Simon went to work. Standing down there between the trees. A young man, nineteen or twenty years old.

When I opened the door, he stood on the stairs just waiting to be let in. Anyone at all, he could have been anyone at all.

Good day, he said. I'd like to use the telephone.

There was something about *good day.* Nowadays there are not so many people who say that, it was more common at that time, in the middle of the nineteen sixties. But all the same he did not say it as if he meant it, as if there were something good about the day, or he wished me that. I felt it seemed like something he simply said, meant for everyone and no one.

We don't have a telephone, I wanted to answer. But that was clearly a lie.

I heard the children from inside the living room. Helena was just a baby at that time, she was lying in a sleeping bag while the other two were playing on the floor beside her. I heard the time signal on the radio, behind him lay the garden, at that early hour the air is motionless, the rain from the previous evening only a slight dampness on the leaves, the green grass, newly wakened, dazed, something quivering in the transition from shadow to the sudden touch of sunlight. I don't know what I was on the lookout for, perhaps an excuse to shut the door.

The connection's not very good, I remarked.

That's all right, he replied. I wondered whether it was up to him to say. Was it not me who should have said that?

We had already been standing there for a few minutes, and the feeling of being impolite eventually made me open the door and stand aside. When I let him in, as he walked past me, I noticed there was an odor about him. It was the smell of a different person, someone who has come too close, and the impression was heightened by my unease. Inside the hallway he looked around, for the telephone or something else. I nodded toward the hall table, but he only lifted the receiver, the sound of the dial tone as he held it above the dial, and the click when he replaced it on the instrument.

He had not intended to use the phone. It was obvious now he had no intention of phoning. What he was looking for, it could have been anything at all.

Nicc housc, hc said.

Yes, I replied.

I had spotted the case attached to his belt, a little container that might hold something, a tool, a folding pocketknife? He must have caught sight of the children then. Greta on her stomach with a large sheet of paper in front of her, concentrating on the drawing, beside her coloring crayons she had emptied out onto the rug. Kirsten's dress had slid up and the diaper she still wore, was visible, she was building a tower with bricks, stacking each one on top of the other. He must have watched them, standing like that looking for a little while before they noticed him, as I felt the unease increasing. I thought I should open the door and ask him to leave, but it was impossible to do so.

A quiet voice on the radio like a whisper, the long branches on the tree swaying in the wind outside, and giving the impression that something was approaching and pulling back again. I have often lain awake thinking about it, the children looking up, glancing inquiringly at him, at me. Helena's arms waving conspicuously above the edge of the sleeping bag. She had been awake for a while, and I knew she would soon start to cry, from boredom or because she was hungry.

I walk past him through the living room door, a reflex making me lift the sleeping bag farther along the broad dining table, away from him, placing it there. At the far end of the room.

He has taken a couple of steps inside, standing focusing his eyes on the girls, the lines Greta is drawing become a big house, a girl with a triangular frock, the sun in the right-hand corner. She is still toiling over a flower.

Why are they sitting on the floor, he asked.

They are playing, I responded.

That wasn't what I asked, he said. The irritation in his voice. I heard it. We are approaching something, I thought, perhaps whatever he has come for. Maybe he intends us to be here, it is here he has wanted to be all along, on this very spot.

Would you like some coffee, I asked in an attempt to avoid it, take a step back to something this might have been, this visit of his.

He shook his head. I don't want anything.

It was not true that he did not want anything, I had understood that.

Helena's waving arms, she was trying to grasp her fingers. Greta who had stood up, who was standing looking at us.

It was a chance I took.

I have some money, I said. And felt how something contracted in my abdomen, it seemed at first he had not heard, or was not bothered, as though money did not clarify anything either. I considered: if he only wanted money. He approached the windows overlooking the garden. The house was the same then, we have not rebuilt it much. Only the garden was smaller, there were several trees, more of the forest extended into the actual garden area, trees we later cut down.

How much do you have, he said as he turned around, standing like a silhouette with his back to the light, his face in darkness.

When I went toward my purse in the hallway, he followed me.

Twenty kroner, I said. That's all.

I placed them in his hand. A pale hand, I remember the hand, I think I will always remember that. He held it out as though he had not thought to take them, just accept them, as though there were a great difference. I noticed it. It was not much, but neither was it a small amount at that time. He thrust the coins into his pocket, and I looked at him, and for the first time had the sense of making eye contact. As though I had not reached his eyes earlier. I felt my heart, it must have missed a beat, thumping against the wall of my chest, faster and faster, unable to calm down again.

I think we both turned around at the same time as it happened. Greta is climbing up on one of the dining chairs, perhaps in an effort to comfort the baby who has started to cry. She tugs the light sleeping bag toward her, the chair tips over, and she just misses dragging the bag with her in the fall. Greta howls, gets to her feet and screams. The baby becomes scared and screams even louder. I console Greta, holding her close to me, rubbing the angry red mark that has appeared on her shin. I lift the sleeping bag. I forget him, forget he is standing there right behind me.

And when I turn around, he is not. He is not there, and neither is Kirsten. For a moment all is silent. The children have stopped crying, the voice on the radio pauses, and only the branch outside the window stirs.

I want to cry out, but Greta is right beside me. I say it carefully. Kirsten, I say, Kirsten. I begin to search, peering around me as though only my own confusion is preventing me from seeing her. Just as I am about to run down the basement steps, I discover that the terrace doors are open.

There is a faint breeze in the garden, I don't know what I am wearing, a thin sweater and trousers, or a dress, perhaps with an apron on top, I used to wear one at that time. The garden is brightening up, I feel the moisture on the grass. At the bottom is the entrance to a little grove of trees. In the years to come we chop down the trees all around, but we leave some standing because we have a notion that the children should see trees, that it is something they need. I walk in between the bushes, into the grove.

She is sitting on a tree stump, it looks as though she is paying attention to something. At that moment she is sitting so motionless that I become frightened, I speak her name. She turns around, looking at me before pointing in between the bushes. Perhaps she has followed him, perhaps he brought her here.

But she seems unharmed. She is sitting on the broad stump and pointing into the forest. As though he has abandoned her and gone on ahead, vanishing in there among the dense branches.

LATER, I CALLED it the episode. When I talked about it with other people, Simon, our children after they had grown up. As though it comes from a place that is unfamiliar, like the intruder himself, a different place. The Greek word is constructed of several parts, of which one part means beginning, like the beginning of a story, a life, but also suggesting something is inserted, in tragedies it is the dialogue that is inserted between the choruses. The episode is the anticipation of something more. But there was nothing more, he rang the doorbell that day, and after that he disappeared.

I know nothing about the intruder. Later I saw a notice in the newspaper, the description of a young man who had entered several houses in the neighborhood, the description expressing the suspicion that he was confused. In a way it was as though nothing had happened. Kirsten was unharmed. But I did not stop thinking about him. Who he was. Sometimes I wake up and it feels as though he is standing in the doorway at that very moment, that I have let him in again. Then it is as if he will never leave, but instead stay here with us. He has just become more indistinct with the years. I must have swapped his face for others. While the incident in itself has become clearer, sharper, seeming to draw closer to me all the time.

The episode that has a hard and inevitable quality when I reflect on it. It is as though it is scored into or through something. A gash, like a tear in thick canvas, in the perfectly normal day, and through that hole something has emerged that should not surface, not become visible.

I OFTEN THOUGHT about it later when I began teaching. He was the same age as my pupils, the intruder. I worked at a senior high school in the city center, an old school. One of those schools with a long-established name and a building that has become rooted in its own convictions, just as unshakably encircled by them as by paving stones and asphalt. The years passed, and I knew that one day it would force me out. The school was sufficient unto itself. I walked around in the corridors, I think I moved around with the suspicion that it was so, that the building considered me superfluous.

I taught Norwegian and for a while literature too, an optional subject that was popular among the pupils. Myself, I was more uncertain. I used to look around the classroom at the pupils, I could hear my own footsteps in the corridors and think that time was passing, and my own excuse for staying there seemed less and less rational. All the same I clung tenaciously to that identity. I was a teacher, a high school teacher. That was how I dressed, how I moved, the role determined my vocabulary, my limitations. As though I could not simply be replaced. And eventually as the years went by the ranks of those of my own age diminished, while younger and better-qualified colleagues continually streamed in. We used to meet at lunchtime, Simon and I, if the weather was good, his physician's office was not far from the school. I walked along Nygaten Street, past all the stores, Allehelgensgate, past Markesmauet Alley, down Peter Motzfeldtsgate to the city park, the Lille Lungegårdsvann Lake, where we sat on a bench overlooking the fountain. We gulped down our food and chatted a little before going back to work. He to his patients, I to my pupils. He often picked me up after the workday. In the car we listened to classical music, conversed about the day that had passed.

If I had a free period and he had cancellations, we could meet at the tearoom in the telegraph building, and when it was closed down after many years, we met at a café neither of us really liked.

I do not know if I miss the work, but I wish to be part of something, I always have the feeling of being left out, standing on the outside. Now that the children are no longer children, but grown women we see only now and again. Occasionally we have been in contact with a few colleagues, from time to time, sometimes a vacation with acquaintances. That was long ago.

For years I stood in the classroom and my eyes scanned what seemed to be the same pupils, all cast in the same brilliant mold after a few years in the building, ready for university. I made out as though I were taking part in it, that is how it feels now. Some pupils distinguished themselves, and every other year there may have been a pupil who was particularly interested, one who did not consider reading Olav Duun to be a personal affront. Perhaps they also became more mature after those three years, I exaggerated the impression of how alike they all became. I regarded them as an expression of the place, everything I personally could not tear myself away from, instead continuing year after year. The work I suspected I was not suited for, was not what I really wanted to do. Without knowing what I ought to do about it. I always said to myself that I was lucky to be able to be there, work there. I used to say I enjoyed it.

And one day I received flowers, and the pupils had bought a special edition of Duun's novel, *Fellow Man*. There were a few words from the principal and lunch with coffee and cake. The days that suddenly altered when I finished. In the beginning it was good being just Simon and me. His gradual change started a couple of years ago. But perhaps his restlessness was present long before that, maybe it is an expression of something he has wanted for a long time. To go his own way.

I CAN AWAKEN in the belief that I hear Simon's voice, the one I am in the process of forgetting little by little as it is replaced by silence. I wake and realize I must have heard it in a dream. It is so rare for him to say anything.

Old age looks out over a gloomy landscape. Helena, our youngest daughter, telephoned a few weeks ago to say she had picked her father up at a bus stop where he seemed to be studying the timetable.

Dad, she had called out to him. Where are you thinking of going?

Where would he go? she asked me after driving him back home.

I could not answer her. I don't know, I said. It's worrying, she whispered so that Simon would not hear. He could have just gone off.

Several days later she dropped by with the envelope and application form. She placed it on the hall table.

I'll put it here, Mom, she said. I saw she was standing in the hallway, in the semidarkness. Helena who was only a baby when the episode occurred. I had forgotten to turn on the light. I found the light switch.

There are homes for the elderly where he would be comfortable. He needs to go somewhere, she insisted and pointed at the envelope as though underlining her words.

A place where people will look after him, she continued. I can't let you take all the responsibility on your own. Now that he's always going off, now that he's so silent.

She spoke for a long time, there was an echo of her voice in the hallway. She doesn't have such a strong voice, but it seemed she had thought about what she wanted to say. And she gave me a hug when she left. She always does that.

A home for the elderly.

I saw that it was lying there. I have left it lying there ever since.

The application form. It is going to occupy my thoughts, no matter what I do.

•

SOME DAYS I cannot remember the distinctive character his voice had, whether it was as deep as I believe, I cannot imagine it. His silence. The words become gradually fewer, as though something is drying up for want of nourishment. After he retired, he liked to go walking on his own, taking the bus into the city and walking up to the university at the top of the hill. Sitting in the old garden beside the Natural History Museum, with the voices of the students from the streets, plants, bushes and trees with their names and species displayed on little signs. Undisturbed, enclosed. Here he sits while the day rushes on across the city and comes to an end with the light sinking behind the trees, behind one of these mountains, perhaps he is reading or just staring at his fingers clutching the book, at the students walking past and giving an impression of sliced movements behind the high, green fence.

I used to phone him when he went out, after a few hours I phoned, and a conversation ensued about what he should bring back, as he usually bought some groceries on the way home. I mentioned what we required, and there was no need for him to write it down, he remembered it by heart.

He has never liked talking on the telephone, I have always been the one who did most of the talking. But a change came about, I did not notice it in the beginning, not for the first weeks or months, it crept in slowly. The pauses, the stillness. He ended the conversations so abruptly that I sometimes phoned back to ask if I had said something wrong.

No, what could it be, he replied. And it was these responses that made me anxious. He always gave the same answer. As though he had a short list of replies he used alternately and held the list up to his eyes, picking out the responses that might suit. And sometimes they did not suit.

He could return home with the groceries, or else he had forgotten them. I said I would make dinner, are you hungry, no, thanks for asking, he might say, or I hadn't thought about it. He went through and sat down with a book, until I placed the food in front of him and he would maybe take one mouthful and then another a while later, until the food was cold and by then it was late in the evening.

His silence came gradually over the course of a few months, half a year. He might say thanks for the meal or bye. He has become as formal as a hotel guest, seemingly as frosty as a random passenger you bump into on a bus. Only now and again do I see him standing gazing out the window or smiling at something he is reading or watching on television, and I think he is back. As though it really is a journey he has embarked upon. But if I ask what he is watching, what is amusing, he just looks at me uncomprehendingly. The physician, one of his junior colleagues, says he has quite simply become old. The solution, for of course there are solutions to situations like this, why should we consult a physician otherwise, is a center for the elderly, a day care center where Simon spends time twice a week.

I drive him. I always drive him places. He sits in the passenger seat of the car and waits until I arrive. The first time we went there, we were greeted by a manager who escorted us along corridors reminiscent of tunnels with plastic walls, pale institutional gray, decorative graphics of anodyne subjects, doors with wooden hearts, and at the foot of one of the corridors a room with glass doors. Inside this recreation area was a little group of people. No one looked up when we entered. The old people sat at a table, two members of staff were conversing quietly. Simon got a chair at the table with the others. He continued smiling. But just as I was about to leave, his gaze followed me. His eyes, hands on the table, the slumped shoulders in that room, in that place. It is not a place where you belong.

When I come out again now, there are often two young care workers standing smoking at the entrance. I have seen one of them drop a cigarette butt on the ground and tramp on it as I walk past. Such a disheartening motion. Several times I have remained standing in the parking lot, like a mythological figure, filled with doubt, this is the border between the underworld and our own world, I walk across the little stretch of asphalt, with Simon in the corridors inside, if I turn around now, he will disappear forever. I need to tell this to someone, how it feels, how it is so difficult to live with someone who has suddenly become silent. It is not simply the feeling that he is no longer there. It is the feeling that you are not either.

I look around the house, everything has its place here too, part of an order. It is so tidy, like a museum or a church, the objects seem to be on display. Few of them do I still have any use for, or have any practical value. They belong to social rituals that are no longer performed to any extent, or if they are performed, rarely have any meaning. They are reduced to a striking series of memories. The old clock above the table, the tea service in the cabinet behind glass doors. It might even be that the house exists to provide a home for these items, to a greater degree than it exists for us.

It was because of the house and all it contains, these artifacts, that four or five years ago we employed a cleaner. I had never had any help before, I did not want home help. Our daughters suggested that we obtain paid help. It is not unusual in this neighborhood. On a few afternoons a week I have seen a little army of young and middle-aged women walking between the villas, letting themselves into the well-protected houses, turning off alarms, security systems. Inside the empty houses I expect they take out washing buckets and scouring cloths, fill them with water and chemical detergents, waltzing around in a miasma of bleach, washing the muck off toilet seats and bathroom floors, feeding pet animals confined indoors, emptying the contents of the trash cans, tidying away toys from the floor in the children's rooms. After a few hours they let themselves out and disappear down the road. I did not want to have a stranger in, but there were no arguments I could use to rationalize this opposition. The girls, our daughters, were of the opinion that we *needed help*. It is a large house, they said.

Simon was not keen either to allow a stranger into our house, into our rooms. He was still the same old Simon at that time. It was before the silence took over. We were agreed that we would do the work ourselves.

But in the end we gave in to the nagging and employed a helper. For the meantime, was the intention. It is strange to use the word *employment* about our relationship with Marija. Although it was of course a form of employment. After a while it seemed far from being anything to do with the relationship between an employer and an employee. The cleaner was more like someone who had come to visit us, a guest we would like to come again.

Everyone liked her. Marija.

She had been with us for almost three years when we had to let her go. Something happened, something that was impossible to get over. When I think about it now, I know it might perhaps have been overlooked by other people. Despite its gravity. Maybe by us too, perhaps we could have ignored what happened. It was the closeness that made it impossible, we had become too familiar. Precisely that she was more like a friend and guest. I think that was it.

The girls were disappointed and angry all the same, the two older ones still are. Although it was over a year ago.

But it was worse for us. For Simon and me.

Dear Marija. I still sometimes formulate that sentence, composing a letter, finding the sentences for myself. I would never write it to her, and I would not write *dear*, not now afterward. If I should write a letter, I would begin in a neutral fashion, with the date and year, and I would swiftly come to the point, whatever that now would be. But why then write to her at all, just to say that she continually manifests herself as a word, a sentence. A glimpse of her can even turn up in my thoughts; I see her sitting in the kitchen buttering slices of bread, drinking tea with sugar and milk, extending her long legs underneath the table and smiling at me. I have tried to convince myself it is more like an obsession, that she still occupies her place here with us, even if it is only a mental place, as when you cannot step on lines, and the lines appear everywhere. You try to think about something else, and the same thought continues to whirl around and around in your consciousness.

I do not miss her. I have a lot to do.

But there is something. Something I miss or perhaps I should rather say lack. She must have served a function, something more than I realized, since I notice this lack. Is that what we are for each other, a function others also can fulfill. I do not like that thought.

I CATCH SIGHT of the empty chair where Simon usually sits and sleeps. As recently as yesterday I watched him. His face, with sleep smoothing out all his facial features, I looked at the shoulders that seem shrunken, and the one leg he always stretches out a little, the hand with the wedding ring. When I left him this morning at the day care center, I felt an impulse to take his hand and feel it, I had the idea that if I held it exactly like that, it would be like an unbreakable bond, not skin and bone, but a different contact, that other contact, the one that has always been there. Before the silence. But I had problems holding his hand, I could not manage it because I was afraid of being seen or of seeing myself in that way. Perhaps it is only me who feels that gaze upon us.

It makes you feel naked, seeking out others and asking for help. Suddenly you are walking along unfamiliar corridors and opening doors. A group of people sits just waiting for you, but no one thinks there is anything wrong, at least anything unexpected. Only this silence.

I recall something Simon told me before he became old, before this irritating silence, that one of the earliest impressions he remembered clearly, was the worn timber floor in the apartment where his family lay in hiding during the Second World War, how the rooms were tiny like boxes with doors, a playhouse where it was rarely possible to play. The walls of brown wood, the roof where he could lie looking up, with a feeling that everything was sinking or being sunk, toward them, inside them, through them, and everything linked to a feeling of guilt the origin of which he did not know, but that probably had a connection with his impatience at that time. The hiding place in a middle-sized city in Central Europe, a place where they stayed week after week, month after month. A place of safekeeping he could not endure and had begun to regard as a threat, since he seldom noticed anything of the actual danger. He quarreled with his parents, his younger brother, he was ten years old and hated being cooped up inside the tiny rooms. It felt as though the world had shriveled, as though it had contracted and would never contain or comprise anything other than these three small chambers, of a size hardly bigger than closets and the few people who lived in them, in addition to the helpers or wardens who came and went.

While they lived in this condition that has to be called imprisonment, Simon told me, they had to remain quiet. Silence was imposed on them, him, his brother, his parents and the two other people who stayed there. Their bodies had already adjusted to a subdued way of moving that never released its grip later, but became part of them, of their body language. They obtained a greater understanding of subtle changes in expression, becoming accustomed to observing others in that way, he noticed how his parents could look at each other as though they were able to transfer thoughts between them, nodding at what the other seemed to be saying; the adults could conduct what appeared to be lengthy conversations in this fashion, simply consisting of facial expressions, fleeting nods or other movements of the head or face, a raised eyebrow, a grimace. It was especially important at certain times of day when there were lots of other people moving around in the building, for example a physician whose office was directly below, who no longer had a large practice actually, but still received the occasional patient. At these times, that eventually stretched out to apply to the entire day, the night, they had really only each other to react to. Simon and his brother. The restrictions, being kept indoors, affected everything they did, everything felt constrained, everything they thought, drew, wrote, and tentatively played. Often these continual irritations degenerated into arguments, insults, quietly and curiously conveyed through gestures, finger spelling, or expressed via furious messages written in chalk on a little blackboard, sometimes with the remains of a pencil, while their parents admonished them in similar silence.

The silence was built in, part of their orbit inside these rooms. At the beginning of course the children posed questions about the curtailed opportunity for movement and expression, while their parents patiently explained. But if one of them, Simon or his brother, was angry and for example began to scream, a handkerchief was held over his mouth, and the feeling of being smothered by this handkerchief, used less as a punishment than through sheer necessity, prevented him from repeating it. Simon recounted that he could still awaken with the feeling of being inside that handkerchief, covering his mouth or being held as a gag. And one day he caused a commotion, by going off on his own. One early evening he had walked through the apartment block of which their hiding place was part, and out onto the stairway, he does not remember how he managed it, but thinks he had escaped by following one of the helpers. It was something he had planned earlier too, without believing it possible. He considered the possibility of running away especially after arguments with his parents and brother. He had planned to go right out, down to the street, but nevertheless came to a halt on the landing. He sat at the window on the staircase and watched people on the sidewalk below, it was a summer evening, people were outside, and everybody had apparently slowed down because of the warmth of the evening sunshine. It looked as though their movements were synchronized in the heat, they resembled waves surging in a peaceful, leisurely rhythm over the paving stones toward the park on the other side of the street. He felt how something of the barrier of anxiety and uncertainty that had seemed to keep him shut off from the street outside, from his friends, school, from recreation activities, the simple ability to walk down a street like this, disappeared. He ran upstairs, opened the door to the drying loft, and heard the pigeons in the pigeon loft close by, the sound was just as reassuring as the sight of the waves of people out on the street, up there he saw the roofs and spires of half the city, and the façades on the other bank of the river, illuminated by a ray of sunshine. A couple of pigeons were treading softly on the ledge. The loft was empty, it smelled of tar, between the bare walls the floor was wide enough that he could have run a few circuits, perhaps he did that too. He kept his eyes on the buildings across the way for a while, the windows on which the sun was still shining, their blinds, their curtains. The people who were probably living inside, balconies with enough space for a family. Simon felt an urge to venture onto the roof, slide down the roof tiles. He opened a narrow window and felt the fresh air outside for the first time in this entire spell he had been kept inside, at least as far as he could later remember. Removing his shirt, he sat down wearing only his thin undershirt and noticed that he was falling asleep. When he woke up, it was to the same feeling of security, not anxiety, he told me. He did not know exactly how much time had passed, but neither had he any desire to know. A car door down between the houses, and yet another. Did he hear it? He still had the same feeling of serenity from his sleep and the heat of the loft when he opened the door to the stairwell. From where he stood on the top step, there was a view out through the stair window down to the street. Two cars, one directly in front of the other, had stopped at the curb on the opposite side. He saw what was happening, that the doors opened, people in uniform, a couple of them police officers, crossed the street, as though one of the waves he had seen earlier was now changing direction and coming toward him. And before the fear, before the dread, he said that he felt eagerness, almost happiness, at the prospect of becoming part of the world down there once again.

Early in the morning I enter the living room and look out at the garden. It is still only a few hours since I drove Simon to the day care center. Recently he has started to eat less, and that worries me. I am trained to worry. The important things are to get dressed, go to the toilet, eat, drink, and talk.

No matter how painful it feels, all that other stuff.

You'll worry, Simon said. He used to say it, before. Always slightly teasing. I wish he would say it now. That I worry too much, that this is not so important after all, just a phase we have to go through.

In the mornings I always try to be the first one up, to steal a march on him, but he needs so little sleep now. He can rise before the night is over or at daybreak, but fall asleep again in the middle of the day. I don't like him nodding off again, and he notices that, for when I catch him sleeping, he always has a book on his lap. I think he does that for my sake, pretending he is reading. We have always read, I used to read Simon's textbooks and he mine.

Before, while he was still talking to me, coming out with more than a word here and there, he used to smile and apologize. I must have dropped off, he said. He still straightens his back when I look at him. The books are always the same ones. History books about well-known battles, especially about the First World War. He has a special interest in that, the First World War and old maps.

One day not so long ago, when he came into the kitchen, I had a feeling he thought she was here, Marija. It seemed as though he looked around and thought there was something missing. Is everything all right, I asked. He nodded, but I think he was disappointed. Perhaps he thought he had heard something, her voice, and then it dawned on him that it was only the radio.

He misses her. He told me that some time after she had gone. Not the work she did, or at least not only that. That kind of work can be done by others. He misses *her*.

The first home help we had was a young girl from Poland. Capable and pleasant, but preoccupied. She used to stand in the middle of the living room and talk on her cell phone, the phone was like an extension of herself, an extra sense. If it rang, she had to run immediately to answer it, no matter what else she was doing at the time. I never saw her without that phone, she talked as if there were nobody else present, absorbed in the conversations, both laughing and shaking her head like a schizophrenic would have done, someone who has exchanged his surroundings for the constant voices in his head. It seemed as though she continually found herself in a public space where people nevertheless did not need to pay attention to one other. In contrast with all the arrangements we heard her make on the phone, she never said a word to us when she was coming or going, she was suddenly standing there in the kitchen when I came in of a morning or appeared in the evening when I was about to go to bed, we never knew when she would be there next.

Lying in the kitchen are the remains of the breakfast and slices of bread Simon did not eat. I pull on my boots to fetch the newspaper and notice that it is going to be a glorious day. The house is situated at the end of a long cul-de-sac with trees on either side. The garden extends around the entire house and forms part of the little wooded area. I was the one who found it when we were house hunting many years ago, I had known for a long time that it was for sale.

I walk to the mailbox, and find the newspaper damp. The newspaper and two letters. Before we moved in here as newlyweds, we had been living for a short time on the other side of the city, down beside the harbors and the massive bridge. During our first days here, we simply walked about from room to room, and wondered where we should place our furniture. All these rooms, all these things. Like the nearby church the house is built of stone, it dates from around 1930.

Both buildings are almost empty most of the time, it strikes me, apart from the few fleeting moments on feast days and special occasions when they rapidly fill up with other people. Holy days. Christmas Eve. Wedding days.

Our name is on the far too shiny mailbox, it was a gift. A present from her, from Marija. The first time I saw her, she was standing right there, with her back turned, beside the old mailbox. I saw from the window that she put something into the box, before walking off. The postman, who was on his way to us, must also have seen what she did, because after she left, he remained standing there and waited for me with the mail in his hand. I think he was pleased. Perhaps at the opportunity to say something he had long wanted to say. He didn't smile, but he could have smiled. He had the expression of someone who wanted to smile.

I asked her, the postman said to me, what she was doing here.

Oh yes, I replied.

She didn't answer, he went on. Perhaps she doesn't speak Norwegian. She might be one of those East European girls who do cleaning. I think so. They're always putting notes into the mailboxes, filling them up with trash.

He peered at the yellow note I was raking out of the box. You should phone the police, maybe she's one of those who shouldn't be here. What do you mean, I said, although I knew what he was getting at. It was an attempt on my part to create a kind of distance from him, what he was, that kind of person. I wanted him to understand we had nothing in common. I have seen him speaking to other neighbors once or twice, he is obviously well liked, although he delivers the mail at his own pace, it never seems to be an urgent task. Sometimes he leaves the lid of the mailbox open, with no regard for whether it is raining.

He shook his head. Now he was staring into space as though a clearer, more meaningful picture was taking shape there. Asylum seekers, he said, without legal permission to stay.

I don't know, I said, turning away and saying thanks for his help. *Thanks for helping.*

Perhaps, he said, checking me with his voice just as I was about to go back inside. Perhaps you should be careful.

It sounded more like a vague threat than concerned advice.

I read her note the next day, coming across it in the kitchen where I had slipped it underneath the microwave. A short printed message. I can help you with washing and house-work, looking after children. Good references. *Phone me.*

A couple of weeks went by before I called.

THE NEXT TIME I saw her, she was standing in front of the bookshelves in the part of the living room we like to call the library, even though that formal name is an exaggerated description of our book collection, which is undeniably large, but arranged in a completely chaotic way, with books in both rows and stacks. She was tall, unusually tall, I remember thinking she was a woman who could lift any man without a problem. She wanted to tell me about herself, she spoke good Norwegian.

She shook my hand. Marija, she announced clearly and with stress on each syllable, as though I would need help to remember it. Her short hair, the side parting and the fringe I remember used to fall over her face anytime she turned to look at me, she wheeled around or glanced upward and her hair would drop like that. A face of the type that people would certainly have called attractive, not too much makeup, aged around fifty or a couple of years younger, I never asked her about her age. Her handshake, a soft hand that did not release its grip immediately. She did not want coffee, but when Simon said he was going to make some anyway, she said yes please all the same. Just a little cup. Always just a little cup. She had a kind of rational modesty that did not seem to be an affectation. This is my husband, I said. Simon.

We agreed she should clean the house once a week, and probably wash some clothes. She seemed pleased, she said she was happy to get as much work as possible. I'm not afraid of working, she commented, speaking in all seriousness.

All the same we were content with the meeting, with ourselves, Simon and I.

I am standing in the garden and feeling the heat. One or two of the windows are slightly ajar. Helena phoned early today, asking if there was anything I needed. I stand there looking at the wide lawn and the two trees at the end beside the low wall, the entrance to the little grove of trees where the intruder may have disappeared.

No, I said to her. I don't need anything in particular.

But now I'm wondering if I should perhaps have asked her to come over, maybe she wanted me to ask her, she has always been circumspect, there was something she wanted to say to me. Her expression is cautious, unassuming, she has been like that ever since she was small, the complete opposite of her two older sisters. She resembles her father, she resembles Simon. There can be so much I miss out on, that I do not understand. The application form she gave me is still lying on the hall table. The application about residential care for Simon. Somewhere he can stay. A so-called home for the elderly. She no longer wants him to stay here with me. If only he would keep calm, she says. And if you had talked together like before. Yes indeed, I miss Marija. It is a lie that I don't, I would have asked her what she thought. The conversations we would have had about Helena, about the recent silence, Simon's silence. All the same it seems as though his silence and her absence are connected. If Marija had never left, everything would have continued as before. I sit down on one of the garden chairs on the terrace. I eat a candy, it seems strangely insubstantial, it does not remind me of anything I have ever tasted before.

Mom, Helena said on the phone. I'm so worried about you, you and Dad.

SHE HAS NO idea that I nearly gave him away once before, many years earlier. How would she have remembered that time, his depression, she was so little then.

It began with some letters arriving, several letters. He found out more about what had happened to his relatives during the war. Almost all his relations apart from his mother, father and brother were sent to extermination camps in the course of the war years. It was only thanks to the hiding place he hated so much that they were saved, he and his parents, his brother. The others are crossed out of history. Friends he played with, girls he liked, neighbors, the man in the store, teachers, classmates, every single member of his mother's and father's family, they are all gone. He felt guilty, I think he felt guilty to be alive, as perhaps everyone would have felt guilty. One day you awaken, and it is like an eclipse of the sun, one of those rare ones when the surface of the full moon covers the sun completely and it becomes dark at midday. You go out with your sandwiches at lunchtime and sit down in the park, beside the lake, looking at the trees, at the texture of the leaves, at the people walking past, now and again someone you know, who perhaps says hello, recognizing you, everything is so indisputably alive, you do not go home, you do not go anywhere. You wish for nothing more than to sit there. For hours. Before someone catches sight of you, becomes concerned and phones somewhere.

And then the dreams. Performances just as clear and transparent as daylight, reproductions of events. They come more and more often when you are awake. The hiding place, the mustiness, the listening silence. The stairway.

He could still feel it in his body, Simon said, the moment on the stairs, as though he were still standing on the stair outside the hiding place that afternoon, looking at the men in uniforms down in the street. Heard their shouts, heard them running up the stairs, at that time when he thought they were surely about to spot him. He is sitting on the same step, not knowing what he should do now that everything is over. The moment lasts, he hears them distinctly, thinks he notices them standing above him with their weapons trained on his head. He looks up, there is no one there. He still hears them, but they are not here, they are in the entry next door, running up the stairs, shouting, knocking, he thinks they smash down a door. He can still see a glimpse of the street through the window. From the corner where he has curled up, he sees a family being led out. An elderly couple, three younger women, a middle-aged man carrying a baby on his arm. One of them drops something, a scarf, a blanket, or a jacket, he sees anyhow one of them dropping something on the cobblestones, and being shoved forward. Simon does not know who they are. He has been shut inside all the time he has been living here in this street. He cannot manage to feel sorry for them. He is relieved of course, although that word is a simplification compared to what he is feeling. In his thoughts this is not only something he observes, he wonders if there is not some kind of connection, a causality between his forbidden interlude on the stairway outside the hiding place and these people, the old couple, a family being picked up by the police. Perhaps he is one of the last to see them together.

•

IT WAS NOT possible to explain. He could not explain it to anyone, it happened so suddenly. The depression. In those difficult periods he could continue for several weeks without being present, without noticing the days pass. I was the only one who knew. Not the children. I haven't told them about it, about the eclipse of the sun. About their relatives, all the people from his past who are gone.

Our conversations about it later, when he had changed his mind and felt that we should talk, tell them. I recall it as a clear picture, an imprint on my retina. I remember he was young, that he was still a young man, and we two were sitting beside each other, he in the driver's seat, I beside him, we were driving along a stretch of straight road with summer cottages and cabins, extensive fields, small gardens, huge farms with barns and farmhouses.

We had been at our summer cottage that day. The cottage was new, and we were so proud of it. An ordinary little cottage by the sea. It had been hard work to pack everything into the car when it was time to drive home. The children, tired out after swimming, falling asleep in the rear seat.

Simon's hand on the steering wheel. I remember it having a pale synthetic leather cover. That bright afternoon. And what he was talking about, the thoughts he was struggling with, that continued to bother him. It was like driving into a tunnel, shutting out the light.

I don't think we should talk about it now, I said.

But when will we talk about it, he whispered.

Once I turned away. I glanced at the girls sleeping on the backseat. They were lying in a heap, their skinny arms, breastbones, knees, brown from the sun. Only Helena was moving in her sleep, her tummy had been a bit sore before she dropped off, like the others she had hauled off her T-shirt and was lying with her top bare, it was before seat belts were compulsory, they were just lying there, as though we had flung them down, almost naked, they liked to snooze like that. The warm August sunlight was shining all around us. Simon by my side. He was wearing rectangular, black sunglasses, a severe style I thought emphasized his gravity when he talked. I did not want that seriousness. I have a memory of turning around and stretching my arms behind me, covering the girls with a sheet because of the open window.

What he talked about. The children sleeping. I wanted to keep it separate, keep them outside that dark tunnel. They are going to want it themselves, he said, to get to know something about it.

I looked around at the stores we were driving past, the tiny houses and gardens. I wanted to be a part of all that outside, that was what I wanted.

They are so little, I said.

Yes, but later, he replied.

He asked if I wanted them to grow up without knowing who he was, his background, the Jewish family. He turned to face me.

I do not remember if I returned his gaze, he had taken off the sunglasses, the deep impression on his nose left by the plastic, or whether I turned away, toward the window. I was scared. I visualized him on the bench in the city park when the darkness descended. I thought of the young women he had told me about, being led across the street toward the waiting vehicle. The baby.

He had already spoken a few times about the possibility of finding out more about his own family, there had been several relatives, a young aunt, a cousin too. He knew nothing about them, no one knew anything about them, what had happened after they had been discovered. They were gone, they were sent off in the same way as the family he had seen on the street that day. Probably for extermination, the atrocities in the camps.

Why now, what good will it do, I think I said. There's nobody left, why should you keep looking?

Once he had shown me photographs of children on their way to a gas chamber, they could have been pupils in single file on a school outing, eight or nine years old and carrying what I recall as bags or small bundles in their hands, dressed in warm coats, but with bare, skinny legs above their shoes. Youngsters glancing at the photographer as they walked past. He had asked me what I thought, how anyone could kill a child. Do you practice in advance, he asked, do you calculate how long it will take? And what do you do afterward. Do you just make your way home?

He was talking about it again as we drove. I thought there was something tactless about it, as though he were being indiscreet, coarse, as though he were relating something inappropriate. It was not suitable.

The movement of the car. Our daughters sleeping.

I shushed him.

Don't drag all that darkness in here, I said.

I don't understand, he said. How it's possible to stop thinking about it.

And when he said that, it felt like a complaint, I felt insulted. He continued to talk for a while longer there in the car, until perhaps I asked him to stop, or perhaps he stopped by himself.

I looked nervously behind me at the children, at him with his suntanned hand on the steering wheel. The August sunlight through the car window. At any rate that is how I picture it now, afterward.

Later, when the girls were teenagers, they wanted to know things about us, they wondered why we never visited any of his relatives. It is surprisingly easy not to say anything, not to tell, to remain silent. I did not want to be part of it. For the girls to become part of it. We told them it had been a small family, we said nothing about the brother Simon had lost contact with, we stated that his parents had been old, they were gone now. Which of course was also true. His parents were already old immediately after the war.

We waited so long to tell them about it. I think we waited too long. By a certain point it had become too late.

I look at Simon and it strikes me that the worry caused his face to age many years before its time, his frontal bone marked with a fine horizontal line I have always assumed to be a scar from his childhood, a little wound that has healed. The kind of scar children get easily when they are playing. But it could also be an expression he often has, a way of wrinkling his brow, that has left its mark.

I found a snail shell. I found it not so long ago in the closet in our room. I do not understand how it came to be there. I opened the door of the wardrobe, and there it lay.

I looked at it for a while. It was one of the big snail shells we see now and again in the garden, a reddish-brown color, beautiful markings, and of course there was no longer a snail inside it, it was empty. The texture was brittle and at the same time somewhat distasteful in such an unexpected place. It was lying there as though it had been placed there deliberately, I thought. As if it were the intention to collect something there, in between the clothes.

I stepped into the living room to Simon, saying: Did you put it there? The snail shell in the closet.

But of course he did not reply. He looked at me seriously, as though he was the one who was worried about me.

I walked back to the wardrobe with the idea of throwing away the snail shell or at least removing it. However, I then thought it had a kind of meaning. Whatever the reason for it lying there, it had a significance. It might be a joke, perhaps he had placed it there as a kind of joke. Would he play a joke?

I do not understand it. And the first thing I thought when I discovered the snail shell was that it might be a statement. It seemed so obvious it was meant to be there, that it had been placed there, like an exclamation mark, placed there for some reason that I did not immediately understand.

Simon had placed it there, I had no doubt about that. I tried to understand. I have continually returned to the wardrobe, peering at it, but I am no nearer any kind of explanation. Now I have decided to let the snail shell be, I disregard it, I have not opened the door for a while. Perhaps I shall simply get rid of it.

The changes in the brain when a person becomes old, the obvious ones, and then all the others. Incomprehensible. It is not made clear precisely what is meaningful when behavior changes. One of his colleagues explained it to me. It is really Simon's profession, Simon used to talk all the time about his profession, lecture me. And there he sat, not so long ago, at a physician's office in the city, while his young colleague examined him. The things they do, efficient and convincing. Things are connected to and fro, cannulas gliding underneath the tissue of skin, machines humming. I watch everything, the rituals, the nuances are as incomprehensible to me as what takes place in a church. It must be because I am lacking in faith.

Once they also took him in for tests. Simon alone in his room, allocated a bed, everything white beneath the intense light, his head seeming too small up near the headboard. I sat beside him and waited. Increasingly more uncertain about what we were there for.

They found nothing. Nothing other than what is to be expected at his age, his young colleague said. He said no more.

It is up to me now to draw the boundaries between the expected and something else.

Something else—a kind of wasteland where one's personality is deleted. This cannot be calculated. I have to interpret him like a recalcitrant poem.

I know I ought to consider the application form. Helena has reminded me about it, but I am postponing it. I look at the envelope, its grave, anonymous exterior.

I attempted to speak to the manager at the day care center, she seems experienced, an older nurse. I have liked her since the very first time we arrived there and she greeted us.

But I cannot make the decision, she said, when I asked her opinion. Whether it was irresponsible to let him stay at home.

I wondered whether I should tell her about the snail shell.

Perhaps it is not classic dementia, she said. And you are the only person who can decide who he has become, whether this is him.

For you are the one who knows him best and who knows, she said. Who he really is.

I WANT SOMEONE to give me permission to do it. To pretend it is not there, this eccentricity. That it can simply be ignored. Even the silence. Then I may be able to tell myself it is not alarming.

But how can I know which characteristics are him. There may of course be something genuine in that, the way he takes off, this stubborn silence. What if it is not that, but the rest of it that was a role he played, that he has now laid aside. And he has emerged at last. Like the girls who appeared from behind the bedsheet they hung up in the living room as children, after dressing up in a variety of roles, in order finally to receive the applause as themselves.

How should I recognize him, my recognition is based on memories, on all those little sequences as different parts of him have become visible down through the years.

Who he really is, she said, the manager.

What you mean, I should actually have said, is who I want him to be.

IN THE FIRST few days after we had engaged her, Marija confined herself to the floors and stairs. She washed the long corridor upstairs, worked on the staircase, audibly discussed with herself what kind of cleaning product would be most suitable for the old linoleum on the stairway leading to the basement, discarded several bottles before asking dejectedly if she could buy a different brand. After only two days I saw her perched on a ladder outside the windows while rivers of soapy water covered the surface of the glass, like a heavy downpour of rain. Her face came gradually into view through vertical lines in the water, she lifted the squeegee and drew it down to the sill, the determined expression she wore when she was working. In the rooms there was an aroma of lemon that I immediately began to associate with her, it became her scent. Surfactant and soap. Pine needles.

We did not like our new role, neither Simon nor I. The more determinedly she labored, the greater our discomfort became. This feeling of contributing to a system that is not entirely regulated, of making use of cheap labor, people without rights.

At the same time we were keeping an eye on her during that initial period, listening to her footsteps around the house, we got the idea that perhaps she was not cleaning the house at all, but inspecting our closets or simply standing talking into her cell phone like the previous home help had done. Simon read an article in the newspaper about East European thieves and left the newspaper lying open at the page so I could read it too. He did not say anything, I did not say anything. It was a shameful little scenario. We probably both excused ourselves by saying we have never been used to having other people in such close proximity.

It also took the form of a kind of guessing game. *What do you think she's doing down there in the utility room, she's been there now for over an hour.* I think we used her as the basis of some jokes too. In the beginning. Would it have surprised her if she had known that? Eventually that passed, it vanished, that initial nervousness or uncertainty, we had let someone in, a stranger. We became used to the closeness. It almost felt like cooperation, although it was by no means that. Curiosity became more kindly disposed. After a while. It took awhile.

One evening after she had left, Simon asked if I thought she had done the same kind of work in her native country. She had commented on a book by an author we both admired. Simon had not expected that, I think it startled him.

I don't know, I said. You ought to ask her.

Shaking his head, he said he could not ask about that, he felt it implied something. That it could be misunderstood.

Imply what you think of her, about this type of work, I said.

No, that's wrong, he answered. He most decidedly felt I was mistaken. He only wanted to know what she did in her own country, the home help. It was not a denigration of this kind of work, or of her.

That's not the way I regard her.

He said.

No, I answered.

But we both knew it.

What lies there. Hidden underneath. Beneath all the understanding, the goodwill. We do not disturb it.

THE HOME HELP and her, perhaps I tried to distinguish the two, make them into two different people. She did not suit the notion I had of home help. Nevertheless: Now that is what I recall, that thing about her height, that she could lift a man, what is that, what kind of meaning does that have. And that she had a discussion with herself about what type of cleaning product she ought to use. It was an impression I had, actually quite comical, but it contains nothing of what I associate most with Marija. Now it pops up all the same. She has become an idea of home help, they are both the same person, is that not the way I see her? But that was not the way I saw her, the way we saw her. The person she eventually became once we had become acquainted with her, there is not so much to say about that. It is simpler now just to view her as the home help. That tall Latvian woman. After what happened.

IT WAS SIMON who phoned to tell them, our daughters, that we had terminated Marija's employment. He used that turn of phrase. He could be slightly clumsy when he wanted to express things, a bit careless. It was an unfortunate way to put it. That in itself must have annoyed them. That he spoke in that way about her, about *having to let her go*. After we had been so dependent on her, after she had been our Marija for more than three years. They were taken aback, he told me afterward. They wanted him to explain why. Marija who had become almost part of the family.

And then they wanted to come home to us and talk about it. Actually all three of them were intending to come, but it was Greta who did. When I think about it now, I see that she has always had the role of the sensible one, the one who takes the lead in proceedings, who puts forward proposals in both camps. I quickly appreciated that she was angry. I guessed that her sisters were too.

My clumsy attempts to express love for them, it has been so important to make them understand, perhaps because of my guilty conscience. About everything we have not said, about what they do not know. They have always been so independent and strong, especially Greta and Kirsten. We were proud of everything the girls did. On Saturdays they used to present little performances for us, cabarets and plays that always developed into wild dance numbers and improvised stories that could continue for hours. They had secrets, we tried to create boundaries for them, give them a good upbringing. We are sitting there watching, they grow up before our very eyes. They are children. Now they are grown up. The girls have always done what they themselves wanted. Apart from Helena, perhaps. I see us in her. Everything we have been afraid of, our cowardice, it has become visible in her. The evasion, the silence.

It was only Greta and I who talked. Simon went into the kitchen to make some coffee. He is so afraid of conflict with the girls. We sat there, Greta and I, she wanted to know why, they wanted to know why, she said. What rules had not been complied with, what could Marija have done wrong.

Her voice had something, sarcasm perhaps, underlying it while she was speaking. She had brought out a pack of cigarettes, opening and closing the lid, repeating that the entire time we were talking. I could see the white patch with the warning and bold script beneath her fingers.

I have my reasons, I said. Dad and I.

But *what*, she said. What could it be?

She has opinions, I answered, principles that I don't agree with.

Don't agree with, she said. What do you mean by that?

I did not know what to say, I was searching for an excuse, a suitable motive, I asked if she knew for example that Marija was against abortion, that she opposed divorce, that she was more fundamentally conservative than I had at first thought. I was vague, it did not make sense. Why should she believe that explanation, believe what I said.

Good God, she's a Catholic, Mom, Orthodox, what did you expect. The house is falling down. You can't manage without that help.

Other people manage fine with what they get, I said. I do not even remember what I meant by that.

Greta looked at me. You've always been like this, she said. Done whatever you wanted.

She thought it was unseemly, she said. Unseemly.

She fell silent. When she started speaking once more, she seemed only sad, disappointed. As mothers can be when they are talking to their children, as I may have spoken to her when she was younger. She had lit a cigarette and opened the veranda door.

I thought you were friends, she said. You and Marija. You don't really have many friends.

No, I responded.

The two of you can't manage on your own. No one manages entirely on their own. I just don't understand why.

WHY. I HAVE placed a blanket across my legs. I have just taken a nap. From the chair I can see the neighbor with his car, his son has come to help him clear out the garage, they are loading boxes and junk onto a trailer. He has lived here since the seventies, his wife moved out more than twenty years ago. He too has home help, a dark, pretty young African girl who arrives in the afternoons. She leaves the house before he returns home, apart from once a month on Sundays, when she undertakes a thorough housecleaning. Sometimes on the weekends he has friends to dinner, and I saw her go shopping with him once. It was only that one time. They were carrying shopping bags out of his car.

But here she is now, talking to the neighbor as he stands leaning against the trailer.

The first time Marija suggested she should come on a Saturday, I was not happy about it. Until then she had mainly come to our house on weekdays. I had confined her tasks to inside the house.

I can drive you into the city, she said, so you can get your glasses organized at the optician's.

Of course she meant Simon's car, he was still driving at that time, I wanted to ask her if she had a driver's license, or if I ought to do the driving, I was unsure whether you could simply and without any fuss take any car and drive when you were a foreigner, even about it being legal or reasonable at all, I was thinking about the third-party insurance. But she had already picked up the car keys.

We drove into the city, we even took an extra turn over the bridge she said reminded her of a bridge in a city she had often visited as a child, she remembered, she said, they used to hang over the railings and fling stones at the seagulls.

Marija related that shc had earlier had a small car she often drove to the university. This was the first time I found out that she had attended university. I was a bit surprised. I know why I was surprised, the home help had once studied at a university in a large city in her native country. She had studied medicine, exactly the same as Simon. But she never became a physician. One of the lecturers, she told me, was an oppositionist even during the Soviet period, an unusual, quite peculiar man. He made you think, she said, like a good teacher should. He was a famous neurologist, and he stood there talking to them at the university and explained the specific connections in the nervous system to them, synaptic plasticity and the axon's growth cone. Had she been a little in love with him? The university was so ancient, she said, that the plaster was falling off the walls, and in an annex they had laid what she suspected were panels made of asbestos cement in the yard outside, the annex was later rebuilt, and parts of the asbestos fell off, but no one bothered about it. I enjoyed it, she said, and so you put up with all that. She said: I liked the smell, you know. The smell of books and the old halls. Sitting for hours and just thinking about one subject. *I read. Everything else was completely immaterial.* Money problems meant she had to give up after a couple of years. She had married, had a daughter. Her husband became ill, they struggled financially before they separated. She told me all of this on that one drive down to the city. She brought the car to a halt in a side street beside the city park.

When I emerged from the optician's, she still sat waiting quietly in the car, her head fallen onto her chest, but I wasn't sure whether she was sleeping, or just listening to the radio.

THE NEIGHBOR SLAMS the trailer tailgate shut and clambers into the vehicle, leaning out to shout an instruction to his son. I look at his home help, the young girl, thinking that she is barely more than sixteen, she lets herself in and hangs his quilt out the bedroom window, busies herself with the housework inside, probably washing his underclothes and tidying his shaving gear. Am I riled, is it the association it brings to mind that provokes me, or is it the displacement of a guilty conscience?

I went into a church. The church is situated nearby, with an avenue of linden trees leading up to an intersection, a field on the left-hand side, and when I turn around and look to the right it is directly in front of me. I have often walked past, as it is one of the places where I most enjoy going for a stroll, and a few times I also stop beside the churchyard. There is something desolate about the way the church is positioned there, and at the same time reassuring. Going inside is not so instinctive, since I doubt whether the edifice has anything to do with me. And all the same I sought it out that Friday morning a year ago. It was late summer then, and the leaves on the ancient linden trees beside the churchyard had the most vibrant hue. The church door was ajar, but it did not seem as though anybody was there. Abroad, in large cities, I have noticed church buildings that are open so people can enter and have a rest, meditate. A place of contemplation. However, this church situated in a quiet spot outside the city center, like other churches is locked unless there are regular services or other special events. Some restoration work was going on at that time. Perhaps that was why the door was lying open. Inside the chilly vestibule I remained standing and peered into the actual body of the church, the nave. There was no one there, only the rows of empty pews and the reredos depicting Christ triumphant on the cross. I have always felt a certain unease at the sight of the interior decoration of churches. The coolness of the walls, the stained-glass windows; everything on the one hand invites respect and yet nonetheless has a somewhat vainglorious quality, intended to provoke admiration. Holiness aspiring to be made manifest through aesthetics. They are also disturbing, these altarpieces. I have always thought so. The faces do not have expressions I can actually recognize, only attributes of humanity, but nevertheless incomprehensible, ethereal. The exalted. But I think more of the anguish that lies beneath. No, I don't understand it. However the severity in this church was transformed, alleviated by the sunlight streaming through the windows on that particular day.

In the center of the room there was a stepladder with flecks of paint and perhaps plaster, and a green tarpaulin had been flung across the floor. I stepped around it. At the same time I heard what I think was a radio. The noise disappeared almost immediately, a door was opened somewhere farther inside, and the clergyman emerged from the doorway. He was an older man, but younger than me even so. I had seen him several times, and had always considered him rather serious and gloomy.

I once saw a movie, or was it a play, in which a woman confided in a pastor. She concluded it all by saying: It was my fault. Guilt is relative, the pastor answered her. Is it? I remember thinking when I heard him say that. I thought forgiveness was dependent on guilt as a given, constant dimension. That only the degree of the offense varied. But of course that is wrong. And the feeling of guilt does not always match the gravity of the crime. It may have been a similar confession he expected, the pastor, when he encountered me in the church that day.

I did not speak to him. He must have seen me standing there, but before he ventured as far as saying anything, I turned away. The stepladder looked as though it belonged there, providing an extraordinary sense of association because it appeared to be illuminated by the windows, it shone and was of course an all too obvious metaphor. As I crossed the vestibule, onto the church steps, a little group of men approached. Maybe they had finished their work for the day, and had arrived to pack up their belongings, they were four older men and a younger boy. From somewhere in Eastern Europe to judge by their conversation, they stood there chatting on the gravel in front of the church steps, only the boy walked past me, he had blue, splattered trousers, and wore a cap over his close-cropped hair, a solemn expression on his face, and I saw that he went in through the church entrance, walking slightly stooped, the doorway was lofty, and he bowed his head all the same. Inside the vestibule he remained standing for a moment, and when he turned around, perhaps to look for his companions, he met my gaze.

ANOTHER DAY WE were walking past the church, Simon and I, and saw a little funeral party emerging from the open church door. The rain had changed our plans to go for a long walk, the linden trees stood somber and still as we strolled along the avenue.

I assume they had already placed the coffin in one of the cars, as all I could see were these few people dressed in black and gray and the open church door. A woman, two younger people and an older man. That was all. And the pastor who accompanied them, he was the one who shook them by the hand. They were so few, it seemed as though they were shivering in their thin garments, in the rain.

Simon also looked in their direction. The place where they were standing.

It is nobody we know, I remarked. But even after we had started to walk on, he turned around and peered at the funeral group. It has nothing to do with us, I said.

I discovered the grave on one of my visits on my own. The year and name indicated that it was the grave of a young man. I thought someone would appear to leave flowers there, someone who simply because of my proximity would tell me more about him, a woman perhaps, or children, parents.

Nobody came. There was never anyone there. I thought the little patch of earth and grass would vanish and merge into its surroundings, after a number of years there would be only a name, with no indication of anything else. Or anyone. The next time I went there, I removed some of the weeds. Last year I also dug up some flowers from our garden, herbaceous perennials which I planted there.

The trees beside the church fascinate me every time I see them. I interpret it as a kind of fortitude that they stand there as always with heavy crowns, despite the road beneath them, and the enormous changes in the landscape over the course of a couple of centuries. These tall trees cast their shadow over the church building, as in the avenue close by. They cause it to appear slightly Gothic as though it were genuinely old. The tower at the front is not very high, but parts of the graveyard directly below remain in the shadow of the actual building in the mornings, it is dark, fertile down there, the green leafy trees seeming to conceal the entrance to another house, one that it is never quite possible to catch sight of. I have also sat on the bench there a few times, occasionally reading the names on the gravestones, or glancing at other people walking around in the vicinity.

The young man. No one knows who he is. Perhaps that is why I have continued to tend the grave. I bring flowers there with me, removing the weeds since no one else does so. At the beginning it felt strange, now it feels almost like a duty.

At odd times I think about what happened to him. Whether it was an accident, whether he himself was careless.

His story is secret, somewhere perhaps there is somebody who knows, I muse, or at least used to know. But time has hidden it, like the invisible house among the leaves. The entrance may exist, but you only occasionally seem to glimpse it between the trees, with their outspread branches.

I HAD A child when I was far too young, seventeen or eighteen years old, the baby's father was someone I hardly knew or even remember, actually he is just as unimportant to me now as he was then. I did not want to have the child, but had it all the same, for a few months after it was born. A boy, healthy and certainly handsome, everything a newborn infant should be.

I am young. I become old when I hold the baby and photographs are taken and the child is sitting on my lap and it feels as though many years go by every night, every day. Before I make up my mind to give it away. For there is nothing about this that makes sense, or that I understand. I am not practical and have always sought refuge in books, in dreams, but this has nothing at all to do with dreams. In retrospect nevertheless it has taken on precisely that character. The birth, the adoption. The months we spent together, when he was still living with me. Now that so many years have gone by, I no longer feel the same responsibility for what with the passage of time has become shrouded in vagueness and ambiguity. I have often thought that I was a different person then. Is it possible to be a different person.

It was several years before I married Simon. I gave him away, I had him for a while and then I gave him away. I do not miss him, I would not call it missing him, I do not know what I should miss, the idea of a child. I did not know him. But I think about him. I see him in different places, there are people I catch sight of on a bus or in some gathering or other, men of the age he must be now, individual features I notice, convincing me that it must be him. Long after he probably would have been grown up, I could watch children coming out of a school and identify boys who resembled his image, the notion I had of him.

I did not miss having him close to me, nor did I regret what I had done by giving him away. But perhaps I was curious.

You love your child so much, you look after it and pamper it, watch out for it, keep hold of it, go for walks in the city, celebrate birthdays, Christmas. Mother. And child. I was not kind to that infant. I was only a child myself and did not think he was kind to me. It was a misfortune that we were together.

BUT THIS BUSINESS of the baby made a powerful impression when I told Simon about it a few years after we had married. He was furious because I had not told him earlier, because it was important, he said, it was something you did not neglect to talk about.

I didn't regard it as important, I said.

How can you say that it's not important, he responded. He was a part of you.

But I do not think so. That this was what he meant to say. I believe he meant to say that it was the other part that was important, that I had given him away.

It was as though he had spotted some deficiency in me. One that he would not accept, as though he had dissected a part of my personality and seen that something important was missing. He thought it unnatural. He used a word like that. Unnatural. A woman did not simply give up her child, and if she did so, she would always feel a sense of loss, and that loss would be expressed in regret and attempts to retrieve her child.

But he has grown up with other people, I said. He belongs there.

He would not discuss it. It was as though everything I said emphasized what was wrong.

Simon tried to explain it to himself. He possessed theories, but nevertheless did not understand it, nothing at all about it. He thought we should attempt to find the boy. He could not understand why I did not want to.

We were at our summer cottage, the girls were little, and we sat watching while they played in the dismal playground beside the nearby campsite. There was a boy there, slightly older than Greta was then, and the two of them began to play side by side. Gradually they drew closer together, and after a little while longer they took part in the same game. I saw Simon watching them intently, watching the boy. When the lad was called over by a woman standing at some distance, who did not even once step foot on the grass dividing the playground from the remainder of the campsite, but almost intoned the boy's name with a certain threatening edge, I saw that Simon took on an expression resembling disappointment, as though he had hoped no one would appear, that the boy would turn out to be abandoned and would perhaps be persuaded to come along with us. He remained silent for most of the afternoon.

In the evening, after the girls had gone to bed, we started to argue. One of the few arguments we have had over the years. I remember I said:

He wasn't even yours. It was before I met you.

He looked at me.

No, he said eventually, you never gave him the chance to become that. Or were those the words he used? It seems too emphatic. Perhaps I have changed them with the passage of time, but I understood that was what he meant. Nevertheless I felt he was less concerned about the boy than about me, about this deficiency of mine.

That night as I lay in the cottage with the rain hammering so hard against the roof that it kept me awake for several hours, I wondered whether it would change. I thought about how he regarded me, with this shortcoming, this part of me that was missing and that he was determined to find again. How can he be so sure, I thought, that it is a valuable part, a worthwhile quality, something worth finding.

I BELIEVE I was pretty for a short while as a young girl. It felt like a distraction. To be looked at, liked by reason of that characteristic, such a debatable characteristic. It never seemed to be something I could make use of for my own sake. It was not worth anything to me, only to others. I knew how I could compel other people to look and regard it as a talent, or something I had earned and about which I ought to be proud. A quality on which far too much importance was placed. In the same way as a disability would have been. Although no one would regard it as a disability. Prettiness and me. We did not get along well together. I did not like the attention it brought me or my own attitude toward it, the significance of it. What it made me.

Simon saw me somewhere, we were young. A look, a dance, we conversed a little that evening. He walked me home, again and again. I sought out the place where we met, a place where young people like us met up, he was there and I remember that we danced a little. We both knew that something was about to happen, but there was a balance, a balance between interest and the trajectory as a result of that, a hand, a glance. A balanced equation. We were trying so hard to be young. He was a dark-haired boy at that time, but older than me, more than ten years older, to me he was a man, his eyes framed by something dark, the lashes, the dark lines I did not appreciate were caused by insomnia, but that made his eyes seem an even brighter blue. In the beginning I could become angry because he had fallen for my prettiness, because it had influenced him, and I was jealous, I wanted him to see me, see who I was, not allow anything so obvious to be a deciding factor. But at the same time I was scared to show him anything else. If there was anything else there. I was not sure, I was young. He said I was difficult, and I finished with him before we had really embarked on anything, I said we should not go out together any longer. He looked at me in surprise. I remember he walked off. Hurt. I thought he would never return. But he did come back. He rang the doorbell. I watched him from the window, he was standing down in the street, and I did not want to let him in. I had heard some people calling him the refugee, but this was long after the war. He came around several evenings, rang the doorbell. At last I opened the door, we sat in my tiny single-room flat. I remember we sat for one entire day in that room, we had never been physical with each other before that. He did not want to go home, because it was about to start raining. That was what he said. And then eventually it was late afternoon and I pulled down the blind, the dark and heavy roller blind that was like a blackout curtain, I undressed, with the sounds from the street outside. I usually undressed by myself in that room, every night, placing my clothes on the chair, getting dressed again in the morning, undressed again at night, the same thing, always the same chair, table, room. There were two of us, we undressed in the dark, in the darkened room. The bed was cold and we were new to each other. We were two shadows, cut out from a different, even greater darkness. His hand traced the curve of my collarbone, across my breastbone, over my breasts as though he was searching for something on my skin, letting his hand glide across. Holding it between my legs, I opened myself up, I can feel it still, that I open myself up, that he is inside me, I miss that, I want him to make me so aroused again, the movement, the excitement, the hot breath between us. As though we were breathing life into each other. A whole new life, into one another. The city and the streets, the old dust behind the window. When I awoke again, I knew that it had started to rain outside.

HE TOLD ME about himself, what city he had been born in, what street, what people had lived there, his family, their names. The background that eventually forced them into their hiding place during the war. He wanted to become a physician, he wanted to be with me. We would have a house, a child. Maybe several children. We won't look back. Is that my idea or his?

I RECALL THAT I had a camera inherited from a relative. A black box you peered down into to capture the object in the lens, never sure that the apparatus would function at the exact moment you decided to take the photograph. I think it places a black wall across the image, dividing it in two, the photo is taken, and the image is hidden inside the box. I also remember the film as a sort of box, a cassette. I have never liked having my picture taken, but I especially recall one photograph that was taken with this box. I still have it, I see my own face on this photo, the midlength blonde hair I cut myself in peculiar uneven layers with the kitchen scissors. I am drawing myself back to avoid closeness, why am I doing that, there is a combination of terror and at the same time contentment in my expression, reproduced almost perfectly in this photograph. There is one thing about this young girl I notice in the picture of myself, something that always amazes me: it seems as though she does not pay any heed to time. At that moment, in the image, there is no past either, I feel. Not when you are so young, not when you are young like in that photograph. Between everything that has happened and everything that happens, there is a dividing line, distinct and defined, like a wall, and the past stays behind that, shut off, forgotten.

In dreams I am often back inside my body as it was before it grew older, I have the feeling of being younger, without any resistance, there is no resistance in this sleep, hardly any sense of gravity. When I move in my dreams, I sometimes have a feeling that is almost sensual. Not that my dreams are. Not in that way. All the same I often awaken with a feeling of desire. Or a kind of yearning that affords a sense of satisfaction in itself. Yes really, it is so. For the yearning does not make me jittery or restless, it feels just like an acknowledgment of something. Perhaps a feeling of closeness to Simon, but the dreams are vivid. I loved it when we were together, simply lying waiting for him in bed, listening to him padding up the stairs, perhaps I switched off the light and noticed as he came into the room, I miss him. It is not so long ago that we were together in that way, but now that he has shut me out, it is impossible. I still look at young men, something in the way they walk, their voices, reminds me of him. When he was young, I wanted him to be older than he was. And now that he is old, that we are both older, I think of him as a young man. Occasionally I have felt a passionate desire for him as he was at that time. It makes me happy, like that feeling in my dreams. Oh but yes, that is erotic. I think I have never been close to anyone in that way, been so happy with anyone as I was with him. That it was so intense. And when I waken, my life, or that part of it, my youth, is like a dream I dreamed just a few minutes before I woke. It was over so fast.

I THINK I hear him talking. It happens now and again. He is sitting in the living room or has gone into the bedroom.

Eva, he says. My name.

I follow him. He might be sitting in his chair or on the settee facing the blank TV screen.

Did you call, I ask. He looks at me uncomprehendingly. I thought you called me.

Or else I think I hear him talking to someone. As though he had answered the telephone. But he hardly ever answers the phone, he lets it ring, on only a couple of occasions recently have I seen him lift the receiver, once he held it against his ear, the caller was probably speaking and had begun to wonder whether there was anyone at the other end, before Simon put it down. The other time, he passed it over to me.

But these conversations I hear. I think I hear his voice, the words are difficult to understand clearly. Once I thought he spoke her name, Marija. I hurried in to him, I think his lips were moving.

Eva.

Perhaps I hear him from the living room, and I go in, and he is sitting with his eyes closed.

I hear his voice, because I want to hear it, a hallucination of sound, like an echo of music or noise that lingers when you have been to a party or concert and return home, as though the brain continues to transmit the sound, as though the inner ear continues to repeat the oscillations, in the place where sound is converted and interpreted as something meaningful.

Eva.

I listen to the clock. It is situated in the living room despite its insistent sound reminiscent of the old grandfather clocks. It seems as though it forces out every single stroke, second, sharp as a hammer blow against hard material, like the workers who were busy outside the church that morning I was there, who were busy knocking something together, or perhaps they were pulling something apart. But the point is that I do not hear it, most of the day as I am pottering about in the house, or sitting in the living room, I do not hear the clock. Apart from a few times in the course of the day, when I suddenly notice it, and when that happens it is difficult to fathom how I can disregard it the rest of the time. Of course I know why, I understand how the brain shuts out impressions that are there all the time, everything that is repeated over and over again, it would be impossible to take in everything at once, always sensing every single smell, hearing every sound, thinking every thought; if the mind did not do so, life would be intolerable. We can concentrate on only a small fraction at a time. Does that apply to your conscience as well?

SOMETIMES WE GO to the cinema. Matinees. The movies vary in genre, comedy, teen movie, romantic drama. I would prefer something different, something historical, but it seems as though these are the only movies shown so early in the day. Simon does not fall asleep, he watches the screen, I think he does that the entire time. The auditorium is almost empty, there are often some teenagers sitting farther back. Several times I have noticed a man who usually goes to the same movies together with his son. He enters immediately after the lights are dimmed, accompanied by a young boy. The youngster is just as tall as his father, I see their silhouettes in the pliant, colored light from the projector as it is reflected back at the audience. Their profiles are similar, he must be the father. But in addition the son has a double chin and his head is too large. The father indicates where his son should sit, they sit down side by side, always near the front, always beside the exit. Just before the end of the movie, as the music signifies an obvious conclusion, the father lifts his son's jacket and makes him bend forward, guiding his arms into the sleeves, as you do only with children, the boy's face is still fixed on the screen and as the first credits roll into view, the father takes the grown-up boy by the hand and leads him out. It happens every time. The young man keeps pace with his father on the way out, but turns around to the screen one more time. The father who is escorting him to the exit before the lights go up. There is a hideous thoughtfulness in his action.

WE DID NOT manage to accept it. This lacking ability to accept an essential aspect of each other. My absent ability to acknowledge his sorrow, and his inability to accept my deficiency of sorrow, regret. He wanted me to recount the story of the child, my love for the boy I gave away. It is not my story, I said. He continued to insist that we ought to search for him. That it would be easier for him as a physician to do so. Eventually he discovered something, via contacts as he put it. A name, a totally ordinary surname, an address not far from us.

Simon thought he had found him, my son. He wanted me to go and look. Meet him. He lives here, he said. He has lived here in this city the whole time, not far away from us. It isn't him, I said. It's a common name. I did not want to go there.

After a while he stopped begging me, gave up talking about it. But I don't believe he forgot it.

An address, a name.

He felt there had to be a common factor between my love for him, for our girls and this story about the adoption. He could not understand that it was not like that. He said that I was fond of the girls of course. I said it was not the same. He could not go along with that. He wanted something more, something else. There had to be something else.

He came out with theories.

When we were sitting up at night, he might start to talk about the boy. He thought it was possible that I had been suffering from depression, women could get a postpartum type. A depression that prevented me from bonding with the child. There was no selfishness involved in that. If I had suffered from depression, it was not uncommon.

Another time, he said something about the boy while Marija was there. A comment, an isolated remark I don't recall. But I do remember I was afraid Marija would get to know that about me, that she would find out about the boy. Perhaps because there would then be two people who knew. Or perhaps because she with her Orthodox Catholic background, or what I persuaded myself at least was such, would consider this an unacceptable thing to do, the adoption. It seems paradoxical when I think about it now. In fact she once found the photograph of my son and me, I had put it together with photos of the girls as children. She initially thought it was one of them.

No, I said.

Who is it then, she asked and looked at the photograph and then at me. And then I convinced myself she perhaps realized who he was. But how on earth could she have done that. It's a boy, I said.

She put the photograph away. I always wanted a son, she said.

We had a dog at the time Marija was here. An old dog. It had been a long time since it had given up regarding itself as a guard dog with the garden as its territory. Now it mostly lay on its woolen blanket in the living room, by the window, the deep tan coloring of its pelt faded, white hairs on the girdle of black around its back, the terrier ears that had been glued when it was a puppy, to train them into the correct shape, still capturing sounds from outside, sounds that were now more a source of skittishness than curiosity. Simon likes dogs. The girls used to say that. Daddy and his dogs.

He was always approaching dogs, puppies. But he did not want to have a dog. It was the girls who pestered us to get Max. Simon repeatedly said he did not want a dog, they ought to have known that.

They went on and on about wanting a puppy. Every birthday, Christmas. Every time they spotted a dog they liked. He became furious, irritated by all the nagging, it was not until long after they were grown up, the girls came home and had bought it and gave it to us as a present. For company, they said. It was a poor show. Simon did not want Max. He said it was a living creature, that they should have asked him. They had wanted to please us, the girls said and were disappointed. It became my task to persuade him.

I tried to talk to him about it.

It's only a dog. You can't blame the dog.

I've given my opinion on it, Simon said.

But it's hard for them to understand, I said, since you like dogs so much.

He did not relent, and I appreciated he had his reasons, the girls would have to look after the dog, they shared that duty for a while. In the end it landed at our house all the same. I went for walks on my own with it in the beginning. He disliked all the responsibility, he said. But after a period of time I noticed him talking to the dog, scratching behind its ears.

I knew that Simon had used to walk a neighbor's dog for a spell as a child. He told me he took it with him on short strolls to earn a few coins. The dog of his childhood had adored Simon. It used to sit outside the door of Simon's home and bark until he appeared, the owner told him it simply ran out into the hallway and sat in front of his door, it never showed such loyalty to anyone else. Everybody on that stairway heard the dog barking and whimpering outside the boy's door. Simon at first did not like the smell of the dog on his hands, the excrement he had to whisk off the sidewalk with a stick. But after a few months of this work as a dog walker—this is how he recounted it to me—he nevertheless looked forward to going on walks with it, he felt more secure, it was far from being a small dog. And later he always connected this dog with his sense of freedom before the hiding place. The walks, the games on the grass. He was certain the dog in some way or other had protected him from danger, such as the neighborhood bullies, the Brownshirts who turned up, that it led him safely from the street to the nearby playground. Its name was Kaiser. Whether it had been a tribute or a joke he did not know. But he remembered his own voice calling out: *Fetch, Kaiser, come, Kaiser.*

The dog we acquired had a quiet disposition, but nothing about it reminded him of that first dog; Max slept on his blanket, ate an incredible amount, defecated in the garden. Simon gradually became more enthusiastic about it, he went on the walks Max needed, patted the dog on the back while he himself was sitting in his chair reading in the evening. But it became evident only after the dog passed away, how attached he, we, had become to it. Simon told our grandchildren stories about a dog he had gone for walks with as a child, but I think these stories were set in a different place, a childhood location that did not resemble the city where he had grown up. In these new childhood depictions everything revolved around this tiresome mongrel he at first disliked, and that sank its teeth into the chain when he tried to lead it around, but later became his best friend. Kaiser. There was no war approaching, no problems.

Our dog, Max, lay beside the chair, stretched out on the blanket, begged in the kitchen, dug holes in the neighbor's garden, disappeared to a place several miles away where a bitch was in heat. When Marija arrived, she complained that it molted, although I never noticed any hairs. The grandchildren called it *Horridandstupid, sit, Horridandstupid, fetch, Horridandstupid, who is Horridandstupid.* Horridandstupid, it answered delightedly to the name and probably forgot its own.

It grew old, its legs and paws were crippled by arthritis, and one day it suffered an epileptic fit, it was terrifying to witness, and affected Simon most of all. It lay on the floor, head banging and body tensing, foaming at the mouth, thumping against the floor. When it recovered consciousness, it attempted to stand up, but could not manage to, it peed on the floor, looking at us, me and Simon, Marija, as though it had never seen us before. The vet talked about putting it down, but we decided we would wait. It should die naturally at home in the living room, on its blanket, it ought to lie there, not on a bench, a table, a floor, it should not die in another place.

Marija used to talk to it in Latvian, she called it by the Latvian word for dog, *suns*. But she did not like it. She did not like dogs. She called out to it only when it was to be fed. It used to watch her from its place in the living room, or stand on the kitchen threshold right until she asked it to leave. They kept an eye on each other. Perhaps she was afraid of it. Maybe a dog has scared her, I said to Simon. It all seemed more understandable that way. She had been frightened. A dog had probably acted threateningly toward her, and it didn't help matters when I told her Max would never hurt anyone. I went for walks with the dog too, and sometimes she accompanied us. The dog on one side of me, her on the other. They never walked side by side. She said only that she didn't like dogs. I thought it was perhaps something she normally said to avoid having a dog prancing about her legs when she was doing the cleaning, I thought she perhaps really did like it. When the dog lay down beside her, I imagined she stroked it. I could envision it, but I never saw it happen. Perhaps I wanted it to be so. When it became clear it ought perhaps to be put to sleep, she asked what we wanted to do.

A dog, she said. You can get a new dog.

I said that wasn't the problem, we wanted that dog.

But it's old, it will go soon all the same.

No.

She said it was different where she came from. Keeping dogs. But I'm not so sure it was anything more than an excuse. Regardless of what the reason was. She did not like dogs.

•

MARIJA SAID SHE thought a great deal about her daughter, her grown-up daughter. She would have liked to have her closer, she missed her all the time. Once Marija was ill and away for a couple of weeks. The house shone following her earlier stint of cleaning, so spotless it might have been sterilized. She always did more than necessary. She had even unearthed some curtains from a closet, old curtains I had long forgotten. Now they were hanging in the living room and gave me a strange sensation of being conveyed ten years back in time, but I liked it.

Eventually the aversion to having help in the house almost disappeared, everything was so well ordered. The wardrobe was filled, the bedclothes hung out to air. The lawn was mown, the hedges trimmed. The floors sparkled. It was no longer so insistent, the distaste about having employed a servant. It had now become essential. This was a wise choice. They all thought so. My daughters. The girls liked her, the atmosphere in the house became brighter with Marija there, they said. We too began to like her, Simon and I. Convinced that it was due to our own efforts, we really thought we were the ones who should be given the credit for it since we had devised the best arrangement, we required assistance, and everyone did the same, our neighbors, everybody in our neighborhood. But we did not compare ourselves with them. We wanted to be gentry of the most pleasant type, making up for all the injustices, the imbalances, we hadn't employed an African teenager.

I don't actually believe we wanted to get to know her. It was not something we chose, but we did come to know Marija. I don't even know why, what it was about her.

You should take better care of your belongings, Marija said. And of yourself. Like a stern inspector, a police officer, she told us what we ought to do. She insisted we acquire a security system. It was installed several weeks later. An electrician showed us how it operated. The security system did not have a complicated program to be followed, you simply needed to make sure you were situated in certain places at the right time, switch on and off, otherwise it would set off an alarm at headquarters. It was not to be fooled around with. Marija said we had to be realistic. Criminals had to be kept out. I think I had told her about the episode. It's possible she misunderstood and thought it was something that had happened recently, that the intruder had forced his way into the house rather than that I had let him in.

She could not appreciate that we had managed without a burglar alarm, and Simon, who had always been against such devices, did not protest, he voiced the opinion that it would be sensible. We wanted to be cooperative, we liked her. Perhaps it was her solicitude.

AND HER VOICE. She had started to shout out "hello" when she came in through the door. I always thought it a comforting shout. Later when we conversed more, she told me about what worried her, about her daughter and her daughter's partner.

She did not like him, he was too controlling, she said, subjecting her daughter to long nights of conversations dragging on and on like downright inquisitions. A child was involved. The grandchild worried Marija. A girl, she explained. She showed me photographs of some people around a festive table, a young girl on her first day at school. A wedding, a Latvian day of celebration. None of the people seemed at all worried. But photographs lie, I know that. On Sundays she wrote letters to her daughter. She consistently ignored all possibilities other than paper, even though I had offered her the use of the computer in Simon's old office, she could obtain an e-mail address. No. But she would like to sit at the writing desk in the living room. She sat there with flowery writing paper in front of her (I'm almost certain it really was flowery), in a pose similar to that of a young girl corresponding with her first pen pals, writing and writing. The letters. The white envelopes. The anachronism of the whole situation was emphasized by her subsequently starting to translate and read aloud parts of these letters to me. Also the replies from her daughter. *Dear Mother, I hope you're none the worse for the harsh winter. Everything here is just the same, there's a lot I can't manage. But soon I'll have saved up a few holidays, I need a break from the whole shebang. There's slush in the streets, you'd think it would have been cleared away by now and that we'd soon have a glimpse of spring, but I think we'll probably need to travel somewhere to find some good weather.* And Marija's response: *Thanks, you mustn't believe that I don't think about you, I do that all the time you know, and as far as slush is concerned, Riga is not the only place needing some dry weather.*

I participated in this communication as though I enjoyed it. Perhaps I did enjoy it too. The details were prosaic, monotonous. Names I did not know, places that were mentioned, people who lived there and their business. Marija tried to explain the connections to me, in one way it was gratifying to stand on the outside and at the same time take part in it all, through these short letter pages, everything described and related.

The infatuation comes slowly but surely. We are so often at home; we sit and wait to hear her insert her key into the lock. Her shouted greeting. *Hello, is there anybody here.* She often brought something with her. *I bought a bag of buns,* or *I picked up a pack of little cakes on my way over.* Her love of economizing led to a lot of cakes and pastries, everything with an almost rubbery consistency, purchased cheaply in a store where they had already been sitting for ages before being reduced in price. She also bought cheese on special offer, and eggs that were about to go out of date. She was aware it was a habit, she said, and begged us to overlook it as a weakness, even though we assured her it wasn't a problem.

Sometimes she baked or prepared some other food, and that was something quite different. Marija was an accomplished and meticulous cook, I think she carried all the recipes inside her head. But she didn't actually like preparing food, she said, she liked to read, she liked to talk about medical studies.

She wanted to hear about Simon's profession.

Marija asked Simon to tell her about the university. She would not have made a good physician, she said, but the orderliness, the scientific building blocks were things she had an aptitude for.

This enormous respect for medicine, that Simon and I believed was linked to some kind of practical-idealistic notion from her upbringing in her homeland. At the same time a form of respect for Simon. They enjoyed talking together. I could come into the living room in the evening, and they would be sitting together on the settee while he showed her something, explained.

We talked about books, she told me about Latvian authors, talking with a pleasure that seemed genuine, with an enthusiasm I thought typical of her, perhaps I am overemphasizing it now in retrospect, like everything I consider to be characteristic of her. Marija liked to make entire stories out of something that could be expressed in a couple of sentences, preferably illustrated by photographs taken with the little camera she carried with her everywhere. To take it from the beginning, she said. That monastery was not here then—but to take it from the beginning.

Simon and I listened to her, listened to the stories that were filled with detail, the tiny details that we pieced together to form a picture of her.

She admitted she was preoccupied by the thought of perhaps returning to university one day. Further studies. But I'm too old, she said. Don't you think?

I said no, of course you're not too old. We laughed at my lie, or what she obviously considered to be a lie, but I meant what I said. Simon and I talked about her having so much vitality, knowledge, despite a somewhat romantic view of art, literature, a peculiar tendency to speak about medicine as though it were a gift of the gods. She ought to study. We were agreed upon that. For a while we actually discussed the possibility of helping Marija. Perhaps she might study at a Norwegian university or we could lend her money to continue her studies in Latvia. But the one time we broached the subject with her, she became alarmed, saying it was only that one period of time, she did not want to study anymore. All the same we didn't give up the idea. I wanted to help her. As though academia were the springboard we would use to save her from the quagmire of humiliation, it can be simpler to be the helper than the one who is being helped, as Simon commented later. I don't remember why he said that. Perhaps we needed an excuse because we never helped her in any way at all. But it was an outrageous remark. We must have seemed so patronizing, we were convinced we were different from the other people she worked for. As though our attitude, what we actually wished to be, made all the conditions of her employment so much better.

THE DOG HAD started to deteriorate at this time, it suffered a number of fits, and in the end it would no longer lie down, or sleep, or rest. Its sight was already affected, and its balance. It was unable to sleep for several nights, we gave it a sedative that worked for a short while until, unsteady from the medication, it resumed its restless wandering from its blanket through the house from room to room, bumping into things, swaying, losing its balance and staggering onto its feet again, walking right into the glass door leading to the terrace, as if it were attempting to walk through without paying any attention to the glass. I thought it was wandering about because it was afraid to lie down, afraid to drop down into the darkness during the fits. It was easy to imagine its helplessness, and in an effort to escape the dog paced to and fro, to and fro, peeing on the floor beside the bookcase, tottering into the closet, into the table, thrusting its head against the cold glass of the door, becoming entangled in the curtains that draped themselves over its back like a shroud. It moved backward in an attempt to release itself from something it could not identify, sat down to gather its legs, struggled to stand up again, set off on the same round-trip. The blanket, the bookcase, the closet, the hall, the kitchen, back to the living room, the glass. Over and over again. Never lying down, never taking a break. It did not recognize us. It stared at us, the eyes, or the expression in the eyes, seemed human, it was the gaze of an old man, a woman. A child who has just had a ghastly nightmare. Who awakens, who are you, why are you doing this to me.

In the end we had to tie it up outside the house, low moaning that after a while turned into loud barking. The barking that used to indicate pleasure. In the early hours I watched him stand or try to stand, with his neck turning ecstatically from side to side, looking in the direction of the road as though he had spotted something, perhaps hallucinating, half blind. Seeing someone coming. But no one appeared.

At six o'clock the dog had been standing like this for two hours, it had started to rain, and I had been outside and tried to drag it underneath the shelter of the eaves, clapping the wet coat, drawing the dog's body close to mine, but it was reluctant, it did not take long until the dog was out in the rain once more. I put on my slippers, went outside and talked to him. Now he seemed more disappointed, it must have dawned on him that no one was coming, his barking had become quiet and complaining. I unleashed him. He immediately resumed his wandering, the same stiff, mechanical gait with his neck thrust down between his legs and his coat saturated with rain, straight ahead now, across the terrace, over the driveway, along the road. I lay down to sleep, I was exhausted by the hours between being half asleep and wakefulness, the howling, the barking, I fell asleep and did not wake until nine o'clock, with the feeling I had overslept. Simon, who was first up, asked if I had seen the dog.

I told him I had let it go.

He looked at me. Waited in the doorway, looking at me without accusation, as though this was something I had to discover for myself. I couldn't let it in, and it couldn't stay like that any longer, I said.

He nodded. But there was no agreement in his gaze. We knew that I had killed it, it had not happened yet, but we knew it. By eleven o'clock it had still not returned.

We searched, Marija as well, and when we spotted Max standing by the side of the road down beside the highway two hundred yards from our house, I was certain it sensed we were there, and that was why it attempted to cross the road. There was not much traffic, it was a Sunday. It wanted to cross, its fur plastered to its skin, to its body, it was skinnier than I remembered it had been at any time before, it started to walk, and I don't think either of us noticed the car approaching. The vehicle was driving slowly. Perhaps that was why we thought the dog had plenty of time, that it would make it, perhaps the driver also thought it would have reached the other side long before, but then the dog changed its mind, and the driver was not fast enough. It moved backward, but was hit all the same. The dog withdrew toward the side of the road again, looking down at its leg that seemed to snap, its head following its eyes downward, it fell, slumped, collapsing onto the gravel. Max lay motionless before we managed to cross over, he looked at me, I recall, with an expression of surprise, I placed my jacket over the dog's body, though I don't think the gesture meant much to him. Marija took my hand and Simon's hand, held them both, we formed a circle, a little circle around the dog. She talked to the driver of the car who was repeating over and over how sorry she was, that she hadn't seen it, that it hadn't been easy to spot. Her children inside the vehicle, she must have forbidden them to come out, because they were staring at us through the rear window. The dog's death had been so distressing, so dramatic, Marija made coffee and sat with us for the entire afternoon, evening, listening patiently to stories about a dog that probably had little to do with the real dog, the one that was now gone. She did not once say we could get a new dog, she said nothing. She listened, and I think Simon wept.

•

I DID NOT believe, I have never believed that I was cowardly. But what does it mean to be cowardly, it depends on what you are confronted with. If there is something you do not really fear, then you are not a hero. There is always something you are truly afraid of. For most people cowardliness is measured by what you risk losing, weighed against the thought of losing yourself, is that not the way it is?

Marija liked to hear Simon read. He used to read aloud to me from the newspaper. He has always been good at reading aloud. He has a rich, deep voice, expressive. No, I hardly remember it any longer. It is disappearing all the time.

When he was reading she used to come in. Perhaps she had been standing in the kitchen, but when she came in and stood in the doorway in order to listen, the seriousness in her expression, even when he was reading lighthearted subject matter. And corrections. He has always had an obsession about correcting language, he would come in from his workroom just to read out a mistake he had found in the newspaper.

He never corrected her. He knew perfectly well what it was like to try to master a foreign language. It took him far too many years to put aside his own accent, his own minor linguistic errors. She didn't know that, that he too was not from here, from this city, from this country, that he too had once had an accent. He never told her that.

•

ONE MORNING SHE had arrived early, she had let herself in, I wasn't even aware she was there. I came out of the shower and was about to walk down the stairs. It was quiet in the house, I don't remember where Simon was.

It came to light later that she had spilled water on the stairs, she was on her way down with a full bucket. The old linoleum was as slippery as a skating rink, I took one step and felt myself lose my footing. It happened so quickly, just an assortment of movements running into one another, a dance devised by an unorthodox choreographer. I had a feeling of being hurled out in midair and then landing beyond the steps.

She came running up from the basement and knelt down beside me, feeling my feet, my arm joints.

It's not painful, I said. But she was already trying to help me up, as you do a patient, she supports me, almost lifting me into the bedroom, I hang on to her tall body, as I'm carried off.

I am laid on the bed. It's all right, I say, to reassure her. I was lucky.

She is talking about phoning for the physician. She lies down beside me. Her feet stretch out beyond the bed, she is so tall. She holds my hand.

I need to hold it, she says. I feel it was my fault.

It's my own fault, I tell her.

No, she says.

We lay like that. I fell asleep after a short while, I saw her face in a landscape resembling a garden, a confusing collage where she obviously did not belong.

Are you sleeping.

I awoke.

No, I said.

She lay looking at me.

It was lovely to lie there with her.

She began to talk, as usual about her favorite topic, about her daughter and her prospects. Still she held my hand. She did not let it go until I said I wanted to get up. I thought: We are so close.

I can't explain why. Why it was Marija. But it felt as though we had been waiting for someone or other. From loneliness, or simply boredom. Perhaps she reminded us of the girls. We let her in. It felt as though we had been waiting for her all the time.

I THINK ABOUT that morning, and it is almost as though I forget everything else, now it all seems strangely unfamiliar, and I am just as astonished as my eldest daughter was when she stood before me that day and asked why, what was it that happened, what meant you could not forgive her.

I wake all of a sudden. I must have dozed off in the chair here, and now I have that heavy feeling I sometimes get when I drop off during the afternoon, as though something existential, fundamental, has risen to the surface and lies just below, about to reach my consciousness. But the only thing I feel is sadness. And I can't manage to grasp what was almost so clear to me as I was on the verge of waking, and consequently there is nothing I can do about it, no way to make it disappear again.

He found someone. A relative, another survivor. What year was it? The children were almost grown up, I didn't even know that he had been looking, that he was still searching. Irit, she was called, Irit Meyer. A second cousin about his age. She was a widow and lived in Germany, in Berlin.

We visited her a year after they resumed contact. We traveled to what was then called West Germany, we took the train and stayed with her for a week. The train journeyed through Trelleborg, Sassnitz and the German carriages had a distinctive odor we both noticed as soon as we boarded. Like leather or burned rubber combined with the sickeningly sweet stench I suspected might emanate from the toilets, something that might explain a more synthetic element, such as liquid disinfectant. After we were halfway through the journey, our hands smelled too, the jacket I placed over my head in an attempt to get some sleep seemed as though it had never smelled of anything else, and I thought that everything was going to be permeated by that odor, our clothes, including our luggage, our hair, our very beings, once we had reached our destination.

For a while we shared a compartment with a young woman I thought spoke no Scandinavian, English or German. She boarded at one of the smaller stations. She placed her suitcase and bag on the rack above the seats and brought out a book, all three of us were reading, we had no need to talk. The silence between us was not uncomfortable. It was more like a gesture. Although we probably would not have managed to make ourselves understood in any case. We nodded to her and she nodded back, as though we already knew one another well and had chatted together for a long time. As though we had reached a stage you normally attain after a lengthy friendship.

Beyond the windows glimpses of various landscapes disappeared, stretches of cultivated fields and villages with clusters of houses. Without dismounting from the train we were transported on board a ferry where truck drivers congregated in the cafeteria. We went there too, Simon and I, we drank our coffee and then dived down again into the bowels of the ship where the railway carriages were situated. The ferry tied up at the quay, and after a longish interval with screeching metal from the steel wheels scraping against the substructure, booming noises and spasmodic movements, we emerged into the daylight again as the carriages were linked together, and immediately afterward we were on our way.

Toward the end of the journey the train rolled into a station, a voice said something incomprehensible on a crackling loudspeaker. We listened for a while, the voice seemed to die away.

A couple of minutes later the door to the compartment was pushed aside by an East German border guard, one of the young men we had already seen on the platform. On his head he was wearing an idiotic uniform cap, far too big, pulled well down his forehead, the brim hiding his eyes, while the crown sat proud as if it were padded out with a flat sheet of cardboard and covered with material I remember as green or was it beige. His gun was undoubtedly somewhere near at hand, though I don't recall seeing it there in the compartment. I noticed his high boots that on his skinny legs seemed as overstated as his uniform hat and contributed to the impression of a rented theatrical costume.

He looked at Simon and me with an expression suggesting we were his main priority, that we were the ones who had made it necessary to visit the compartment. I was sure he would ask for our papers that I was already holding in my hand, and at the same time suspected this would not be sufficient to satisfy his demands. But it was the other woman he directed himself toward, the one who had shared our compartment and the silent friendship. He lifted a magazine she had left lying on the little folding table below the window.

She had been sitting bent over the same book for most of the journey, now she resembled someone who has been wakened and does not understand what is going on. She glanced at us, at him.

He started to talk, no, shout at her with an almost unintelligible accent, or perhaps it was the volume that made it almost impossible to understand anything of what he was saying. She withdrew into her seat, she was obviously scared and probably did not understand either what he was trying to say. He held up the magazine and continued to scold her for what he clearly regarded as a filthy, undermining glossy rag. We just sat there and watched him shine his flashlight up at our luggage in the already fully illuminated compartment, he made the woman move, we thought he wanted to look through the rest of the luggage. We saw how she had to turn around several times, an absurd four-step ballet under this man's gaze. I was afraid for Simon, that he would get himself involved, that we would be thrown off the train on the wrong side of the border and forced to find some way of crossing over to the West. But just as quickly as he had started, the man in uniform ended his reprimand, closing the door again behind him, controlled and completely calm now, showing no sign of his outburst of rage. Through the window in the compartment door I saw him talking to a colleague, just as quiet and levelheaded as if everything had been playacting. The woman sitting with us was holding her hand over her eyes. Simon tried to say something to her, something comforting, but she simply acted as though she did not understand and took out her book again. Her hands were shaking, our hands were shaking. We resumed our attempt at reading. The silence that had been so reassuring was difficult to endure now. It began to grow dark outside, and I saw the reflection of our faces reproduced on the glass, in the train window. Pale in the harsh light of the compartment.

WE SPENT A week in Berlin, I had soon begun to feel homesick. These were a few days during which I just felt superfluous despite the second cousin trying to do all she could to make me feel at home. The city and its air seemed almost damp in the heat, especially the asphalt, the wide sidewalks down beside Kurfürstendamm, the dampness mixed with the warm smell of the asphalt, as though it were about to evaporate and become incorporated into the clogged, dusty city air. In the Zoologischer Garten a male lion was wandering restlessly around in a depressing cage behind glass, forced to live out his life as an exhibit while hordes of schoolchildren walked by. I stood observing it for a while, the roars that were intensified by the acoustics and did not sound as though they came from an animal at all, but were more reminiscent of the noise from a building site I had noticed several blocks farther up, where the machines appeared to be shifting boulders backward and forward before dropping them in a seemingly arbitrary location, this snarling of the machinery and occasional rumblings, a terrible almost supernatural sound. Or even the growling racket from the underground train we had taken a number of times, the so-called U-Bahn, that when it passed through a tunnel beneath the earth, made me think more of a monster who in the unbearable heat and afflicted by insomnia was trying to hide himself in the darkness.

THEY DID NOT talk together only about the war. They talked about the time before that, when they had both been children and spent several weeks together at a holiday resort. It was memories from that time, and about being children they talked about with greatest pleasure, they liberated themselves from all the years and found their way back to something different they must once have been, she related that she had gone through a little childhood crush on him. She remembered Simon as the irascible second cousin, she said, and she had wanted to marry him, but someone had warned her that you didn't marry members of your own family. For a short time this information had bothered her more than the approach of war. She described the holiday resort he had almost forgotten, relatives he barely remembered now, names she could help him with. She was involved in some work, an organization that searched for the identities of so-called displaced persons who filled Europe after the war, and that attempted to chart the precise fate of those who were victims of the Holocaust, and what had happened not only to them, but also to their traces, their property, what was left behind. His second cousin, or "dear cousin" as I heard him call her, as though he was trying to bring her closer than she actually was. Perhaps this is what is difficult to understand. I am jealous. During the visit I sit in her living room as she tells stories, she serves coffee, she dishes up some tiny round cakes that look like cookies with a sweet filling, and she puts her arms around me, cradles me as though she is comforting me, as though I am the one who needs comfort, as though we are old friends. She does the same with him, and he is so delighted, he can't get enough of her and her anecdotes about the family and the past and everything that has vanished; he has got his name back, Shimon, she says, his face is transformed while we are there, he slips into the old language and the stories of his upbringing, it feels as though I cannot breathe in that little apartment, so close to the past. I go for a stroll in the little park beside Viktoria-Luise-Platz. I sit there for several hours. But I have to return, although I don't want to. On the stairway I fumble in the total darkness until I find the little light switch that has to be pressed, and as I do so I feel an excitement, an anticipation immediately before it happens: For a fleeting moment the entrance is illuminated, I see that the entire wall is covered in tiny square mirrors, paintings, decorations, a manifestation of art nouveau. I walk slowly up the steps watching a mosaic of my own face, what appears as a never-ending series of versions, all of the same stairway, of reflected images and an extension of the staircase that apparently reaches as far as the roof. Immediately afterward and just before I stand in front of a new door, and as the light is extinguished behind me, I open it and wend my way back to all the other things. The darkness in the hallway, the clothes hangers, the photographs in the apartment. The past.

•

AFTER THAT SHE phoned now and again, Irit Meyer, but it was her letters that arrived most regularly. I didn't like them writing to each other, I never liked the letters and the conversations about the time in their homeland and the holiday resort and the past. Why didn't I like this? When she rang, she always talked German to me, I tried to reply with the little I could muster of the language, that Simon had taught me. German is a language where it seems you can speak a whole chapter to the conclusion, sentence by sentence, without inserting periods or indicating who and what is being spoken about, until the very final syllables. The actual contents are elegantly packaged, like the yolk inside an egg, you crack it carefully on an edge and the contents run out, self-assured, sticky, but beautiful and rich, down into the bowl. One says that one has seen, one has had some thoughts about. *Man hat sich Sorgen gemacht.*

In the conversations with Irit they came to life again, he said they came to life for him. His parents of course, but also other relatives. The younger aunt who had lived with them for a longish period together with her little son. One of his father's sisters. When he thought back, he was less concerned with her, she was part of the adult world. The adults he knew as snatches of conversation, good and bad weather; the grown-ups gathered around the table in the living room with cherry wine or anxiously huddled around a newspaper, heads close together as they sit looking at an article, reading about new regulations, about war brewing.

But then the aunt had a son aged five or six. His cousin was more indistinct. Irit Meyer remembered some things. Fragments. The boy's family had come to visit on some of the vacations, he liked to spend time on the beach, liked the sand, the waves, but he was shy, she thought she remembered that he collected things in his pockets, she thought it was him, but he had lived for too short a time to leave any deep impression. There were a few sketches remaining, some children's books, she thought there might be some photographs. Simon recalled that his aunt spoke very little, that during the time they were living together, she was preoccupied with her husband who had gone under cover because of the work he had been involved in, he stayed away permanently, although the intention had been that he would come and live together with them. She altered clothes, Simon had a clear memory of that, she fixed the clothes when you were growing, he recollected the strange feeling when she measured him, the length of his legs, his arms, he stood with his arms exactly as she had instructed him, perhaps he liked her firm and at the same time careful hands. His aunt recorded the measurements in a little book, she always had a suitcase sitting there, she never unpacked properly. He remembered that suitcase. And also the contents that he glimpsed on the occasions when she opened it to fetch something or place something inside. The suitcase was important, it was always ready. Like a warning, an imperative long before anything took place. Several times he had wanted to sprint out into the street with it, put it down in some random place and leave it there.

He remembers two things: The cousin has a visual impairment, he has strong glasses it is forbidden to touch, without them he would just stumble around helplessly, and if he gets milk, something there is very little of anyway, he becomes ill. He vomits on the kitchen floor, the smell permeating the entire apartment. Simon comes into the kitchen, and there is vomit on the tablecloth and across the floor, his cousin has been taken behind a curtain to be washed. It is a curtain made of hand towels. Behind that curtain is a tub of water, and there are voices there, probably his aunt, the young mother, talking to her son. He remembers it like that. He remembers everything else so perfectly well, but not his cousin. Only these two commands. Don't touch his glasses, don't give him milk. That his cousin's glasses should not be touched is something Simon has been told by his mother, probably also that he is helpless without them, for he has no memory of that, no picture in his memory of his cousin at all. He is hidden behind the curtain of towels, he only pops up in his mother's admonitory voice about his glasses, the sight and smell of vomit, the open windows in the tiny kitchen. Simon is confused, he can't recall anything about this boy, he searches in the photographs his second cousin sent, rummages through the words he believes he has heard.

It was as though he avoided being seen, he told me. His cousin was small, he sometimes sat by the window, his face directed out toward the street. No, that was himself. Simon sat looking out the window and down into the street, he loved to look out the window. He thinks he waited while his cousin was on the toilet, heard him in there. Does he ever come out? He goes past him in the dark passageway, the cousin looking away, they take a photograph, the cousin stoops down. But in one or two of the photographs he is visible all the same, a newborn in a blanket, a tiny speck bundled up in another lighter speck.

HE HAS MORE dreams about his cousin later. A shadow he knows must be him. He almost always dreams the same thing, Simon says. He is in the old street where he lived as a child, he has been inside the old apartment, his cousin is waiting outside. Sometimes the cousin is a child, sometimes he is grown up. When he is a child, he is sitting in the enormous tree in the yard, a tree that is much larger and sturdier in the dream than Simon remembers in reality. Simon walks by, his cousin shouts, he calls out something, but Simon does not look at him. He thinks it is a dreadful thing to do, but he will not stop. It is even worse those times when the cousin is grown up. Then he is standing in the courtyard outside, they meet and take each other by the hand, say hello, sometimes the dream starts when he is going down the stairs, Simon says, and he knows there is something he wants to avoid, he searches for opportunities to leave, but there is no opportunity, he has to go out the same door, out into the same courtyard where his cousin is standing, good day, they greet each other, his cousin takes him by the hand, walks by his side, but the cousin isn't going anywhere. He asks Simon where he is going. And Simon is going to work, that is what he says. His cousin asks if he can accompany him. If he can come with Simon. Yes, Simon answers, because the question is like the narrow passageway, there is no other response, no other possibility, but nevertheless he knows that his cousin cannot tag along, and therefore he has to come up with a lie, and in his dream he is sweating, he is wriggling away, he has to run from his cousin, but can't manage to do so. He awakens, lies there feeling as though his cousin has taken up residence within him. He never actually sees his cousin's face now either, it reminds him of others, it is complex, it can't be brought out of the dream. But then the dream or dreams change at some point in time. Now the cousin as child and adult are interchangeable, he stands there like a beggar, child, adult, old. And he always wants the same thing and Simon knows that it's not possible, he can't keep company with this creature, ghost, *Gespenst*, that is what he is. He says that. You can't come with me. No, he says. Why not, his cousin asks. Because you are dead, Simon answers. The cousin looks at him, and appears to be just as alive as everything else Simon senses exists in this dream. You died as a child. How? his cousin asks and is so young, old enough to understand the words, but not to comprehend. He is eight or nine years old, older than he was when he disappeared. Simon cannot answer. I don't know, he says. His cousin asks if that is why he cannot come with him, if that is how it is. Yes, Simon says. He wakes. He falls asleep again, he dreams the same thing, with only small variations, with only small changes. He has this recurrent dream for several years. It constantly torments him. Sometimes Simon thinks he sees his cousin when he is awake too, he says, sees him someplace or other, in the background, in a corner of his own field of vision, but when he tries to turn around, he is erased. This ghost, this intruder.

I phone Helena and invite her to come over, I need a few groceries. Yes, that is something she can help me with all the same. If she has time.

She seems pleased. I can do the shopping, she says. Just tell me what you need.

After twenty minutes I hear her car driving up in front of the house.

It's me, Mom, she calls out. As if it could be anyone else. And then she says no more for a few minutes, before standing in the kitchen doorway.

The application form, she says. It's still lying here.

Disappointment. Her face and her voice, her hand with the letter.

She gives it to me. And now I have to open the envelope, I have to look at the sheet of paper with the blank spaces where Simon's name should be. I have to say oh, I have to say I must have forgotten about it. I have to find an excuse, she is right to be displeased with me, she has taken over that role. It is the intention that I should feel ashamed.

I'm a bit disorganized, I say and apologize to my daughter. She says it's all right, Mom. Fetching my glasses, she places them in front of me on the table and puts the grocery bags on the counter. Sit down in the living room, Mom, I'll sort out the groceries. I go into the living room and put the application form down in front of me on the coffee table, closing my eyes as Simon usually does. Open them again. From the window I see a flock of sparrows gathered on the terrace. The radio is playing the Beatles. It must be the Beatles, Simon likes them, he has never been too old for the Beatles. What's that called, the song they're singing. "Michelle." It's a long time since I heard that. Simon should have been here now.

The newspaper is lying folded on the table. She is busy tidying up out there, opening and closing the doors to the fridge, the kitchen cabinet. I read the newspaper headlines upside down, managing to read a whole column, a whole paragraph. I watch the sparrows. *Michelle, ma belle, these are words that go together well.* Simon loves that song.

Or am I the one who loves it.

Do you remember that book Dad liked so much? she shouts. The history book.

I know what she means. His great hobby, battles of the First World War. She is still standing in the kitchen, shouting.

Yes, I say.

I promised him I would read it.

Michelle, ma belle, sont les mots qui vont très bien ensemble.

But the truth is I haven't got the time.

Très bien ensemble.

I don't think I'm going to do it, she says, there isn't really any point. Now.

Is it written to a sweetheart, I wonder. The song. It really must be.

I don't understand why they haven't delivered the newspaper, I say. It didn't come yesterday, but today it was there again.

I really should bring it back here with me, she shouts.

What do you need to bring with you, I ask.

She clatters the dishes, putting them into the dishwasher, pushes the door closed. The song is finished, there is someone talking now.

She stands in the living room doorway. Helena, who has always been the youngest. She sits down beside me, stretches out her arms and embraces me, rocking. I accept the sign of affection and hug her back. If you fill out the form, I'll fetch it for you meanwhile, she says.

What, I ask.

The book, she says.

Why does it not matter anymore, I inquire. What do you mean?

I just mean that I won't actually be able to tell him if I like it, we aren't going to be able to discuss that book now.

She strokes her hair with her hand as she speaks, pulling it behind her ears. I can bring it to you, she says. I can come in again afterward in any case.

Yes, I say.

Mom, she says, giving me a hug.

And then she leaves.

SHE WANTS TO return the book she has borrowed from him, as though there really is a rush. An hour later she phones to say that it took awhile to find it. As though I have asked her to do it, as though there is a hurry and it's important. Take your time, I say. I'm here.

But just after that she is standing in the house again. With the book and frozen raspberries she was out picking in our garden earlier in the summer. Everything is contained in two bags. She couldn't be bothered to read it. Although she feels, she says, that he still wants her to do it. The book means something, he was so enthusiastic about that author, the historian who has written it. They talked about it. It was one of the last conversations they had together, when Simon at least spoke a complete sentence to her. Perhaps that was why it seemed so important, she says. She has picked up the book, placed it on the coffee table.

We remain standing for a moment.

I'm always trying to guess what you're thinking, Mom.

Are you? I say. You know I talk all the time.

No, she says. You don't.

I OBSERVE MY daughter, the dark hair, the blue eyes. Exceptionally blue. Simon's eyes. I study Helena, there is something I have always regarded as glassy, brittle, about her. She was always afraid when she was little, afraid of the water, of the attic, of the dark.

Perhaps it comes from the fear she has inherited without actually knowing what she is scared of, could not know.

At one time I must have thought it would protect her. Not knowing, that it would make her, make them, safer. But when I look at her now, it strikes me that it has had the opposite effect. Maybe it works that way, that what you guess at terrifies you more than what you are told. The blurred, nameless apparition.

As a child she invited friends to visit on her birthday. They arrived in starched party dresses, eight eleven-year-olds, stiffly dressed up and critical, going around looking at everything we had in the house, lifting things up and peering at her belongings. No one talked to her, they ate our food, delivered their presents, chatted together in her room without letting her in. She did not complain, I think she was afraid I would be angry with them.

A few hours later, they traipsed home.

I don't know why, there seemed to be no reason. When I asked her, she just said that she was not very popular.

In time she became like me, like us, she began to read, withdrawing more into herself. Her sisters are tougher. Helena is the only one who is a teacher, like me. She teaches science, mathematics, nothing as intangible and vague as literature. I think it is an appealing subject. She teaches at junior high school, I like the thought that she stands facing them, explaining something so solid and certain.

I take one of the bags with me into the living room. I still feel uneasy, perhaps I have acquired her uneasiness. The clock is ticking, suddenly I hear it.

She leaves, and I think about the application form. That she forgot to ask me if I had filled it in.

I REMEMBER SOMETHING that happened once when we were on the way home from a trip to the mountains, just Simon and me, we had been driving for hours, we were on our way down after staying at a little hotel for a few days, it was some occasion or other, and we were driving through a valley that reminded us both of some other place, a place we had been before and enjoyed. We were exhausted. Hungry and thirsty. As we drove over the newly paved highway, I saw a sign saying BYGDETUN, a local museum. I recalled something like this from my childhood, a vague memory of a day spent in the sun at some place like that, and there was the same heat outside the windows while we were driving that day. I said that to him, we could stop, I said. We could get something to eat.

Simon wasn't sure, he drove on, I thought he wanted to pass up the idea. But he pulled onto the side at an exit road and turned the car.

It was later in the day than I had realized, and when we parked the car in the row of other vehicles, I saw that people were already on their way out of the museum, though there was still no sign of anyone dismantling stalls or packing up. Children at one end of a playground were having a good time with a pony, two boys on the stage were trying to grab hold of the microphone, talking into it, splitting their sides with laughter, but the equipment was obviously switched off. There were still families sitting on the wooden benches with thermos flasks and coffee cups. But there weren't many people all the same, and perhaps it would have been different if it had been more crowded, if there had still been a queue in front of the stalls as I expected there would have been earlier in the day, if people had their eyes focused on the stage, at something going on up there. It didn't take long until it dawned on me that we had become an attraction, although that is the wrong word. We were being noticed, or more than that. Passersby were looking at us skeptically, I thought it was skeptically, at least there was no feeling of being welcome. What I had been trying to relive, the pleasure I remembered from the encounter with a similar museum as a child, had completely vanished. Instead I was the stranger, we were the two strangers, who had sneaked into a location where we did not belong.

We continued to stroll around for a while, Simon bought a cup of coffee, I looked at a hand-knitted scarf, I felt I was being watched. Even by the children.

When we returned to the car, we did not speak. We had both, I am quite certain, the same realization of not being wanted. It was a feeling of shame, that we might have misunderstood, read the signs of hospitality so wrongly and believed that it embraced us, that we also without any fuss might fit in and be accepted.

She enjoyed cleaning, Marija told me. As a rule she simply went into a house or an apartment, let herself in with the key she had been given or a key that was hidden somewhere. She worked her way through the house with a mop, a vacuum cleaner. There was nobody there, no instructions. Few of the houses were really dirty. She cleaned just as thoroughly regardless. She saw little of the inhabitants who must live there, who rarely left behind any traces other than an almost invisible hair on the basin, a towel on the kitchen floor, a pair of sneakers in the hallway. Of course also the money that was left for her on mantel-pieces or dining tables, and in some cases, as with us, paid into her bank account. She might discover a coin placed in a strategic spot or a banana skin that seemed to have slipped out of the trash can. A kind of test, she thought.

In one place lived a married couple. At first Marija had thought they were just living together, that he was a relative, or that they were siblings. Because it seemed as though they lived separate lives and seldom spoke to each other, she said. But they were husband and wife. The man liked to sit and talk while Marija went about her work, he chatted about his wife. He nattered about his wife who was sitting on the other side of the wall and who was walking outside in the hallway, between the bathroom and the kitchen, as though she was someone who had left the house and disappeared long ago. Or he talked about their summer cottage and the grown-up children who were there far too often, he rambled patronizingly about their habits, in-laws he could not abide, about journeys they made to places he could not comprehend anyone having any interest in visiting. Every time she was there, he turned up to talk to her. He could sit for many minutes with his observations, talking continually as time passed and Marija tried to work. She had the impression it was not the floors and the cleaning she was being paid for, but that she was actually being paid for conversing with this man, Marija said to me. And there was some kind of inference. Something was being implied through this arrangement. That social barriers were being expunged, something was being assumed that she struggled to understand.

She had the feeling that there might even be an expectation by the two of them, both husband and wife, that she would fill a need that the wife no longer had any wish to satisfy.

Generally she worked alone, although she would have preferred to have the company of a colleague, she liked to have a female friend to converse with. It was often too quiet in empty apartments. But there were always certain sounds that were particular to that very house. She remembered one occasion when an animal was locked inside the apartment next door. Was it a dog, a cat? The sound she heard was so low, a light and gentle clinking, that now and again it might sound like a child, as though a child were locked inside that one room in the apartment, and it was terrifying, Marija thought, that there was a possibility a child was alone in there.

The rooms resembled the pages of interior décor catalogs, she had once tried sitting on a settee, having made herself a cup of coffee using an expensive coffee machine and drunk out of one of the cups belonging to a designer set, she was embarrassed when she confided that to me.

One place was filled with exercise equipment, little else, in the kitchen there were enormous drums of protein powder, and in the living room there were two exercise machines that she dusted every time she was there. In another house there were photographs everywhere of the family who lived there. You would think they didn't have mirrors, she laughed.

In one detached house there had been a spooky cellar, the laundry room was down there, you went down a staircase and along a narrow corridor, and deep inside hung a padlock on the door leading to a dark room, she had peeked in there, and this cellar again ended in a hole, just that hole in the wall. Like a dungeon.

Most of them were ordinary houses, terraced houses, detached houses, individual apartments. I come in, she said, and now I always know where they keep their keys, where they hide them. I know about all the hiding places. Everybody has their own hiding place, but I could open every single door in this city.

SHE MADE FRIENDS with the postman. It was the same man who had talked to me about asylum seekers. Sometimes she used to stand and wait, in fine weather she would stand and wait for the mail, or else she just peeked outside, she had this idea that she ought to fetch the mail for us on Saturdays. It was always the same guy.

I watched her from the window. Her standing on the garden path, and him approaching, walking with his mailbag on his stomach, after parking the mail van on the road. In the beginning I think he barely replied to her, since I saw that she talked to him while he brought out the mail, and that he ignored her.

But later I noticed that they stood together one Saturday and she was laughing, and it struck me that they were perhaps around the same age, he a few years older. Are they flirting? I wondered. I remembered what he had said about cleaners. But now he was standing there chatting nineteen to the dozen.

She waved when he left. She gathered up the mail, turned around and waved.

Simon mentioned his brother once to Marija, she asked whether he had any siblings, she thought he talked too little about his family, she said. And so he mentioned his brother. I was surprised. He never talked about his brother.

I looked at Simon. It was the closest he came to telling Marija about his own past. He said that he missed his brother, that they had lost contact, that they had lost contact after events that—

I thought he was about to say: took place during the war. If he had not stopped at that, he would perhaps have mentioned the hiding place.

She might perhaps have said: Why a hiding place?

Perhaps he would have told her about it then.

However, she interrupted him, saying that there was an effective way of finding missing relatives or others you had lost contact with, that she herself had found a relative, that he ought to try the foreign information service. Simon nodded and smiled, and pretended to be surprised, in a somewhat vague way, yes, he said, he said he agreed, he ought to try directory inquiries.

They are so helpful, Marija said. A woman there told me I only needed to give the name, country and preferably town, but I didn't have the town. And all the same, only a few minutes later I was talking to Milda, and we were both overwhelmed. Milda and I who had not spoken to each other for many years.

EVENTUALLY MARIJA TERMINATED several of her work arrangements because she was tired out. The last time she was in the country, she had steady cleaning work for a storekeeper and ourselves. Only sporadically did she take on other work in other places. In places she described to me as attractive apartments, all of them almost empty.

It was so easy to work there.

Norwegian houses are clean, she said. Like Norwegians.

I laughed. But she was quite serious.

It's true, she said. Norwegians are. Always beautiful. And clean.

SOME DAYS HE simply goes to the car after breakfast, installing himself in the passenger's seat and waiting until it's time to drive to the day care center. If I haven't followed him after about ten minutes, a quarter of an hour, he presses the horn. It varies how long he waits, once when I came out he had fallen asleep. He presses only once. If I don't arrive, he sits for a while longer, and if I still do not come, he opens the door and struggles to stand upright again. Gives the door a little push. He walks disappointedly back to the house. At least he appears disappointed, his expression is grave and reflective. He never asks why I haven't come.

He goes out to the car. Waits. I let him wait.

He will not speak, I will not drive. He sits in the car for almost half an hour. I see the back of his head from the window, it strikes me that he is sitting too quietly, in a moment I will make a move to run outside, but then he moves.

He comes in again, sitting down on the chair in the hallway without removing his overcoat, he looks through the hall window, staring out at the car. I say nothing.

I look at him. I think about what he would have said.

Usually I come before he sounds the horn. I sit down beside him. Sometimes he gives a satisfied little snort, and camouflages it by lifting his pocket handkerchief, he wipes himself continually with the handkerchief now, it might be a habit from his childhood he has resurrected, as though someone or other, perhaps his mother, might be standing over him telling him to remember his handkerchief. When I leave him in the corridors of the day care center, it still feels as though I have abandoned him for good, as though the entire car journey here has had the aim of placing him and leaving him there while I make my way as quickly as possible to the exit, and escape.

Before I leave, I always kiss him on the cheek, his soft skin, and feel his cheekbone beneath my lips.

ON THE DAYS he is not at the center, he wants us to drive. He does not say where he wants to go, but I know that he wants us to seek out places we have visited before. He seems contented then.

I drive him.

There's a pleasant smell of leather in the car, no matter the time of year it is always snug and secure, I have the feeling of being in a house, a movable house that has been built around us. Most often we go nowhere.

The drives started many years ago, but they had a more fixed purpose at that time. We were on our way to the cottage, or to visit my relatives, one of the children who was studying in a different city, or some of his colleagues. We still sometimes go on extended journeys. We drive out of the city, perhaps the sun is striking the roofs of the passing cars, a stream of cars. Soon, up in the mountains, they disperse and disappear, only one or two will follow us farther up, but then they too are gone. It is spring, almost summer or fall, early fall. He often sits with his head sideways, resting on his shoulder, he is sleeping or just leaning his head there. His gray hair against the seat fabric, the heat of the car. Previously he was often the one who drove. We would talk about things we saw, sometimes it was a river coming up on one side, meandering its way down the valley. The water and the earth beneath appear green, a turquoise color, and in one particular spot it is like a whirlpool, churning, an agitated movement, as though trying to run the other way, against its own power that draws it downward. Other rivers are clear and slow, melted glass running over stones, perhaps the valley stretches itself out in front of you, no people, only grass, a derelict, transparent house, the walls disappearing, soon only a framework remains under the roof that disintegrates stone by stone. A pile of glass, an accumulation of materials, a defective angle, a distortion of the surrounding landscape. The loneliness that exists in some places. It is impossible not to be moved by it. It happens so abruptly. Maybe we have been there before, maybe he says that, maybe we talk about it, an everyday conversation, music on the car radio, voices coming and going. I remember we liked to sit and listen to the radio. But that is the past. The trips we take now are without purpose, we do not talk, we don't really go anywhere, and it is just the trip for its own sake. But recently I have had a feeling that we are nevertheless bound for or at least looking for something. We drove through the forest a few days ago, and while we were still inside a canopy of leaves, it struck me that this, that the forest I saw, was an inherited visual impression, that it had always been there. Of course not seen through a car windshield, but the same picture in any case. In contrast to the asphalt road, the road signs, the exit roads to picnic areas. While I drove he sat beside me sleeping, I wanted to wake him, I wanted us to see this together, that we should talk about it, as I think we used to do. Or did we only talk about the children, about work and the house and finances. I don't remember. But I felt it so strongly, it was something quite special. I began to consider what it was that was going on inside him, when he sat like that with his eyes closed, once sleep had taken a grip on him.

Sometimes I collect him early, he does not seem to have anything against it, he comes with me, and I help him to put on his coat, and instead of driving home I steer the car out onto the highway, we drive out of the city, through the tunnels and all the way out to an open space where we must choose which way we are going to drive up into the mountains. That is where you end up regardless. Then I turn around and drive back. And one night I lay close beside him, it was a dream, but I heard his heart clearly, the skin like a fine membrane and he fastened his arms around me, I pushed him up in the bed, until he was almost sitting, I climbed on top of him, pushed his erection inside me. While I did that, I noticed that I was crying. When I glanced at him again, it seemed as though he wanted to say something, but he could not manage to articulate it. I sat up, I tried to help him, there was something stuck inside him, I felt for his pulse, and when I did not find it, I moved over to the other side of the bed and pressed my hands, the palms of my hands, on his chest. He opened his eyes again as I was doing this.

When I awoke, he was lying by my side, and I sat up and felt for his pulse even though he was breathing just as softly as usual.

I was at the church tending to the grave of the unknown boy, Simon was helping me to water the plants with the watering can, when the pastor approached us. He spoke just as quietly as I had expected from someone like him.

He said that he had seen me in the church that day, he had seen me go out again, and it was a pity we had not been able to have a chat. If there was anything I wanted, he continued, then I only had to get in touch. I gazed at his face and thought he was perhaps saying that out of a sense of duty, but he seemed sincere.

I'd like to mention that we have a baptismal service on Sunday, he said.

I nodded, I thought to say: We probably can't manage that.

On our stroll that Sunday we noticed that there were small groups of churchgoers gathered outside the church. We peered over at the open doors with people going in and sitting down. During the service Simon closed his eyes, are you sleeping, I asked, but then he opened them again. As though he needed to shut everything out only for a moment. The child to be christened who was carried to the front by a round woman with a midlength skirt and shiny, black boots, what shall the child be named, its hat was taken off, its head held over the baptismal font. Just a few more inches farther down with the child's head, hold it under, then it would be a completely different and terrifying type of ritual. The family stand in a row, all in their Sunday best, the child is silent, it is a boy. A girl is singing, a young girl, a psalm, an unbelievably high and delicate voice, a doll's voice, she is singing the psalm "God is our refuge and our strength," is that what it's called? Out on the church steps Simon took the pastor's hand. I did not believe it usual for clergymen to stand on the church steps. But Simon took him by the hand, he grasped it, held his hand tightly as though there was something he wanted to say, and I think the pastor was waiting for that too.

But no words came. I saw that the pastor was waiting, Simon smiled.

He could have been smiling about the pastor, about anything at all. It seemed that he was considering something.

The clergyman nodded to us in farewell.

When we went away, it came. The word Simon had perhaps been thinking about on the church steps. Brilliant, he said. It was the first word he had said in two days. Brilliant.

•

I THOUGHT ABOUT it afterward, whether it was just a word that occurred to him. Occasionally words crop up, as though he stumbles upon them, he finds them and it appears that he explores the meaning, feels them, whether the meaning is still there, whether they are worth articulating. Other times it seems as though they take him by surprise just as much as they take me by surprise. Bankrupt, he said one day. Photocopier. Calligraphy. He peers at the newspaper and reads fragments of a text, assault, care of the elderly, tax evasion.

I thought earlier it was the beginning of something, I waited for the next thing he was going to say, and a whole day might go by. I was sure that the disconnected words could be part of an expanded monologue, that just took place over time, and that there was something in particular he wanted to express. Like the story about two trolls, or is it three, the one says something, then a hundred years pass, and the other one replies.

If I pick them up, his words, and put them together, might the collection add up to something, give some kind of meaning. Or perhaps not.

I WAS IN a church as a child, Simon told me many years ago. He had two memories of this church. The first was one ordinary day, before the war, a small gang of boys was wandering around aimlessly. Simon, his little brother, a friend, maybe one or two more. The group stood in front of the church that was located in a quiet street. They were the only ones present, there were no adults in the vicinity. And the church that none of them thought appeared impressive, it was just like other churches, a cruciform church, built in the shape of a cross, a construction based on the Latin cross, in which the central nave is long. It was situated on an open square, with a few houses and other buildings on the outer edges. No one watched over the church, why should anyone watch over a church, they are on a reconnoitering expedition around the building, a massive stone edifice with gray ashlar, and the tall tower, the spire. They have never been inside. This building that they must have seen before, but perhaps have never paid attention to, has become the object of something not yet formulated, waiting to turn up, to take shape inside their thoughts. What if they scrawled something, spat on it, what if they climbed a tree and clambered onto the lowest section of the roof or carved a message on the church wall. None of them has anything to write with, no chalk. That is when the eldest of them opens his trousers. Shocked and excited they observe, understanding his intention, what he is planning. But his fear makes him unable to pee, only a couple of sparse drops emerge and settle as a tiny stain on the pale wall, at the foot of the building, beside the staircase. They stare at the dark stain, is it possible that it's growing, spreading outward, that it's forming into a complete picture, a pattern? The eldest boy is still standing with his hands on the waistband of his trousers, the sun shining on the dark stain, and they hear an orchestra playing in a side street, not long before the war. A church.

A man in a dark-colored coat comes up the street, an adult. They start to run, they sprint as boys can at that age. Across the public space, down the street, vanishing over the cobbles. They will never return. At that time the very thought causes Simon to awaken in fear at night. On a couple of occasions later he walks down that street, and every time he has a feeling, he relates, that the stain is visible, that it continues to spread outward, just waiting to be noticed and it is only a question of time, soon it will be visible to all, the entire city.

THE VISIT OCCURRED awhile later. I went there with a female friend of my mother's, Simon said, someone who subsequently also helped us to find the hiding place during the war. He said his mother had to overcome her pride in order to accept assistance, there was a conflict between her and one of the helpers, a conflict that had arisen because of him and this visit of his to the church. I remember her vaguely, he said. The female friend. Perhaps her hair was brown, perhaps she wore it long, to her shoulders, perhaps her upper teeth were slightly protruding, slightly crooked, perhaps she smiled with her crooked teeth and dark red lipstick, and her long hair lay on her shoulders and swept over them when she turned her head, the people from that time are so evasive, he complained, the simplest characteristics elude memory, although individual traits stand out distinctly, almost overexposed in one's memory. Such as that she was carrying handkerchiefs and continually picked at my clothes, he said, hairs, tiny specks, particles of dust that were lodged there. It was this church she liked to frequent, she was probably Protestant, he remembered there being a Protestant atmosphere inside the church. She is a woman or girl in her late twenties, a friend of my parents', he said, it is easy to forget they were quite young themselves, they became old so quickly after the war. Although I don't have any reason for knowing it, he continued, I am convinced she did not have any intention of converting me. She was just sharing a story that engrossed her, and the church was the place where the story would best be told. Through her knowledge and understanding both the Old and the New Testaments became a multicolored parade, and her low voice a cast-iron bridge over which the entire story proceeded into his more than appreciative child's brain. She retold the Bible stories with intensity in that voice, sad, beautiful, grotesque, loud, what else. Simon used words like that when he talked about it. And then there was the actual visit to the church.

Perhaps it is a morning, or perhaps an evening, there are the enormous windows, the pictures above the altar, the anticipation, the church organ. The organ music slams against the walls, Simon is sensitive to noise after several ear infections, but he tolerates it, is not tempted to stick his fingers in his ear canals in order to muffle the sound, there are other children there like him, maybe they believe he is her son, he believes himself that he is her son. Perhaps he stands up with the others, folds his hands like they do, imitates their gestures, what is it they are articulating. No one folds his hands or prays in his own home.

Had she asked him not to say anything, invented some reason so that the grown-ups in his home would not know about it? It had to be a secret between them, and therefore he saw it as their story. The angel, the Christmas Gospel, Golgotha, the Crucifixion, the Resurrection. The church building from outside looks like all churches, molded and massive, like concrete, although it might be older, ancient, even beautiful, but she sits beside him and holds his hand, and once during this period of time there she stands up and accompanies a little flock of people up to the arch in front of the altar, she has signaled with her hand that he should wait, and he does so and notices that the other children do the same. While the children's parents walk forward in a disorderly line along the floor, they kneel, lean forward and kneel as they receive something into their mouths. He thinks it is something good and is slightly disappointed not to get any, it is seldom that anything good is handed out.

But afterward, when they leave, she explains to him that it is not as he thinks. He walks along and holds her hand, she is almost solemn as though she has made a conquest, he imagines, as it now strikes him as an adult. He thinks they stop at a café and he has something to drink. Lemonade, tea. He is contented, she continues to tell him about the Testament, but when they approach the house where he lives, she asks him not to say anything to his brother, he might be jealous. Perhaps not to your parents either. Has he intended to tell them? No, he hasn't.

The visits, for there were several, were discovered. The book he had kept hidden under his mattress too. The New Testament that he had read and regarded as a fable with magicians and wizards. The New Testament that I hadn't exactly swallowed and digested, Simon said, but that had at least made an impression, especially the story about the Resurrection, about the women at Jesus's empty tomb, I liked the parts that seemed like magic, although I am uncertain why I associated it with something so cheerful. The Crucifixion, how it shaped itself into some idea of an exciting fairy tale. It must have been the way it was told, how Mother's friend told it to me. It devastated them. My parents. The visits and everything it must have led to (what it had led to, he did not know) enraged them, not because they were religious, on the contrary, but because in their opinion she, their friend, was trying to give me something fraudulent, something that did not belong to us, Simon said. It was not the religion, but the lack of respect, neither of them being particularly religious, but it had to do with identity, his father said. Who they were. Who are we, he had wanted to ask. Mother who was angry, Father's face, sad, old even though he was still young. He did not believe in anything. Simon has never believed in any testament either, but he told me about this memory with pleasure, he had been taken to a place, it was secret, like a secret show, a performance. He walked past the church several years later, the church building was dark and closed then, there was nobody there. He still remembered that the doors had opened, the candles, the organ, the theater stage. The whole sparkling story. Brilliant.

In the stores and on the streets down in the city there is movement that I miss otherwise. I have become one of those women who view the world from bus seats, out through windows. From park benches and waiting rooms. I disturb no one and am not disturbed. I can go wherever I want without being obtrusive, my body is hardly visible within a group of people, I am neither fat nor thin, neither quiet-spoken nor loudmouthed. Should I make more of myself? After a few hours in the city, it's like being inside a churning, whining machine, and when I return home, I am grateful for the silence as an insomniac would be for sleep.

I think up different tasks to do in the hours until I have to collect him. Sometimes I go around the house without finding anything to do. I can stand for ages staring at the clock and without noticing it lift my hands to my mouth and then feel the contours of my face, just standing there like that as I stroke my face with a repeated motion until I become conscious once more of what I am doing. I look at my body and it dawns on me that I should be satisfied now that it does not express anything other than what I am, that I no longer need to relate to a beauty I cannot stand for, a type of femininity I have never felt entirely comfortable with. But my body gives me more validity, the physiology, the machinery, is more conspicuous than ever before. Everything that was hidden and displaced to the background is taking its revenge and has moved into the foreground, the malfunctioning lubrication of the joints, even peristalsis, the bowel movements that mark the times of day more clearly than any other events, there is a certain comedy in that. It is genuine. At the very least you cannot claim it lacks authenticity.

The clock that strikes so loudly, but right now the sound is not insistent. I open the door to the living room. Directly behind it is the chair where he usually sits.

Some days I almost forget his silence. Then it feels only like a momentary stillness, and that we are going to talk together soon. He is going to say something, and I am going to answer. How I miss it. I want to tell him to stop doing this to me. It feels as though it is something he has made up his mind to do, something he has chosen of his own free will. That he has shut me out, all of us out.

When we had just met, it kept crossing my mind that he was going to disappear. That one day he would sit in a train, or perhaps on an airplane, and find another place far away from me, from us.

He would leave a note, a letter. I would open it and read what he had written. It would not explain anything.

Later he told me he had thought the same about me.

I have come to realize how the voice, the words, are the way into him. But also to us. It feels as though he has withdrawn, he has closed himself off. In the same way that traffic is blocked off in the old street where we used to live when we were newlyweds, the traffic was diverted and the street deserted. It feels as though he is in a different house, a place I cannot enter, I see that he walks around in there, something he smiles at, he is busy with various things, I notice all of it, and he looks out at me through the windows, he stands in the doorway. At a distance.

A FEW YEARS before the episode occurred, when we had just moved to this part of the city, and Greta, our eldest daughter was a baby, I used to go for walks. On these walks I began to notice a boy in the neighborhood. He did not live close by, but on the other side of the field, not far from the church. He always walked on his own to and from school, without any friends. I was often out with the baby carriage at the time school finished for the day, and then I saw him walk along by the lake. He took his time. Stopping and peering at whatever there was to look at, there were several older boys there at that time, who were constantly flying kites. He kept an eye on them down by the water's edge. I think that he was the same age as my son, the boy I gave away. It is like a game, in which you know all the time that you are creating the idea as you go along, you realize it is not real, but that has nothing to say for the illusion. I liked the notion that he could have been my son. It gave me a kind of reassurance. It was a comfortable thought, that he had done so well for himself, I must of course assume what I saw of him now meant that he must have done well for himself. I could envisage an upbringing for him, just nearby. A family of three, I saw the house where he lived, a house with a garden, in winter he probably skated on the lake, and in summer they went on visits to their cottage.

I went alone for walks in the evening and saw a light on the second floor in the room where he stayed. I spotted him at the window. He was sticking something to the upper part of the window frame, a little figure hanging by a fine thread, it began to spin around, perhaps in the heat from a radiator directly below. We both stood watching how the movement, the figure, went one way and then back the other way. Him behind the window and me outside, at a short distance. I had a feeling, or I was sure that, he was aware of me. At least once some time had passed. My restless wandering to and fro with the baby carriage.

The all-too-accidental encounters. On one occasion, he was with his parents. I glimpsed him a couple of times in the schoolyard too, when I was walking past the school. Saw him with his buddies, and on his own. Another time I noticed that some boys crossed the street in front of him on the way to school, pushed him or tripped him. The group had dispersed by the time I came on the scene. He was on his knees, his heavy schoolbag preventing him from getting up.

Are you all right, I asked. He just nodded. I helped him to his feet, and when he looked me in the eye, there was no gratitude there. He hurried down along the sidewalk, and I remained standing watching him, Greta in the baby carriage started to cry, as though she sensed that I had forgotten her for a while, she continued crying until I picked her up.

Later I walked past him on the sidewalk.

I persuaded myself that we had a conversation.

He looked at me. I looked at him.

Are you all right now, I said. *I would have liked to talk to you.*

I don't know who you are.

No. But I would like to explain.

He stopped making eye contact, I noticed that he was walking the same way as before, but more frequently he walked down along the lakeshore. When we bumped into each other, he always hurried by.

•

WALKING PAST SOMEONE on the street, looking at his face, seeing where he lives, knowing the route he takes every day, for example going to school. Looking at him going over, watching him cross at the same place every day. Noticing his features, such as that his face is young and unformed, that he is perhaps ten years old, perhaps twelve. He is only a boy in the neighborhood. There is the house where he lives, there is the school he attends. Here is the road he takes, sometimes he walks along by the lake.

I have often thought about him, I try to find his face, hold it fast in my thoughts, the face of that boy. He has nothing to do with the episode, in the same way that he has nothing to do with the boy in the grave, but all the same it has taken on an association in my thoughts, as though their shapes are superimposed on one another, and again I think about a photograph, a photograph that is overexposed and shows two subjects, melding together in an accidental combination. As your memories always do in your consciousness.

I WAS UP in the churchyard one day, and there was another woman there, a woman of my own age. I noticed that she paused for a moment beside the grave. I felt curiosity about who she was, whether she could tell me anything, I wanted to talk to her and rushed to approach her, but when I reached the spot, she had already started to move away, and the more I think about it, the less certain I feel that she actually stopped beside the grave. That she stopped there longer than beside any of the others. She was probably searching for another grave, perhaps she was simply a person who went about reading the names on the gravestones.

Why does that unsettle me so, that absence of love, of care. The loneliness of the name and the little pile of earth. That no one comes, that there is never anybody there. I remember when I was a child and accompanied an older relative to the churchyard on Sundays, a little graveyard hidden away behind an old church, I used to play there as if it were a little park while my grandmother tended the graves. She took care of the dead. She seldom told stories about them or described their lives, there were few details available except for the ones who were placed in clear view on the walls of her house, framed portraits from which those who had passed away stared back with hazy eyes, but there was care in the way she picked stones from the earth and carefully planted fresh flowers among those already growing there. It seemed as though she tucked them in with the dark, heavy soil between her hands, in winter she removed the snow, and around Christmastime she lit a tapered lamp that she left sitting there when we went home. As though the dead also needed light.

I HAVE THE application in front of me, I have let it lie on the coffee table, I think I creased the edge of the paper when I removed it from the envelope. He is old, it is best for both of us that I give him away. Helena thinks that we have talked about it. Don't you remember, Mom? That I ought to give him away. Have I talked about it. I can't remember that. Her sisters probably agree. It's likely they are behind it, pushing her forward on the makeshift stage in the living room. She began to cry, it often happened that she started to cry. She tried to do what they wanted. She should dance, it was a part of the performance. Or sing, tell a joke, perform a conjuring trick.

Make him disappear. They have decided. His stay at the day care center is not enough, he needs a better facility. A *home* for the elderly. I must appreciate that. Our solidarity has something suspect about it now, something presumptuous.

Simon who used to sit in his chair and sleep for hours, he can in the afternoon. I look at him then and wait for him to awaken. Occasionally he says something in his sleep, but it is nothing I can manage to make out. When our daughters were children, I looked at them sometimes too when they were sleeping, they could fall asleep anywhere at that time, on my lap, on a stair, on the bus home, in the back of the car on the way home from a late party, or as on that August night on the way back from the cottage, it always happened suddenly, they went from being wide awake to fast asleep in an instant, as though they folded themselves up, spinning sleep around themselves like a larva spinning itself into a chrysalis, their eyes slid closed, and it was almost impossible to wake them until several hours had elapsed, and when I looked at them, the thought passed through my head that I actually did not know them. In sleep, during the hours they forgot us, I thought about what harmed them every day, what was shaping them or was in the process of shaping them, what they were afraid of, which I did not know about, had no notion of figuring out, but perhaps was visible to them inside there. I felt so helpless. They seemed, and still seem, so close to me, but nevertheless they live their own lives, I don't know if I know them so well. I used to think: Whom do they resemble, what family traits are visible in them, features from people long gone. The application form on the coffee table. I have found a pen, the pen has the logo of a hotel chain, a telephone number, the address of a Web page. I have no idea how it has ended up here. Who has left it on the table?

Surname, it states, please use capital letters. I put a dot on the sheet of paper, it is blue. Think I hear Simon breathing out. Previously he often breathed like that when he wanted to say something, like an exhalation to gather strength. But he is not here. It is my own breath I hear. I stare at the pen, and at my hand holding it.

THE BOY I gave birth to, my son. I have thought about how I watched him lying in his own bed and sleeping, waking. Sleeping again.

I rarely lifted him, only when I had to feed him or change his diaper.

Otherwise he lay in the little cot, and most of the time he cried. Variations in crying, from quiet sobbing to a terrified, loud scream, a howl. It went on for hours until the weeping eventually died away and was replaced by silence. In the daylight I could see streaks on the skin of his face, they resembled scars. His hands were often clasped together. He could look at me with what I interpreted as fear, I believe he was afraid of the dark, the sounds from the street, perhaps he was afraid of me.

He drank the milk I gave him from a bottle, always restless, always a movement from his arms or legs. As though there was no place to find respite.

When he was a few months old, he attempted to lift his head and upper body, to rise up, perhaps he was peeking out looking for me, or maybe for a way out, but in the same way as someone at the opposite end of life, an old man fettered to the bed, he was getting nowhere. He let his heavy head fall back against the pillow and mattress.

The crying.

It continued. It was all he had. He became big enough to sit up, looking at me with the same scared expression, his eyes flickering. I can't recall him smiling, but I never smiled at him, so it was never noticeable.

I wanted to give him away immediately, but someone, I think it was one of my parents, had said that since I had him and had landed myself in this situation, then I must take responsibility. And so I sat there with him. He wanted me, but I did not want him.

There were other moments too, perhaps when he was sleeping, perhaps when he looked at me without wanting something, that I could experience peace, when I did not feel shame and anger, that it was not so bleak. I sat up one night with him when he was sick, the pediatrician had said I had to keep him up, I was forced to sit with him on my lap while he slept, stirred, fell asleep again. When he awoke, he looked at me and I at him. For a second I thought he was about to smile, something at the corner of his mouth.

I lay him down in his cot again, perhaps from anxiety. Scared that he would change something, that he would push his way in, find a place inside me and claim it as his own. That he would stay there without me being able to disregard it, his insistence, his screaming. I let him lie. He screamed and screamed.

The times I took him out with me, I went for a walk in the park, or let him sleep in the baby carriage out in the backyard or down at the foot of the stairs.

He was perhaps five months old, and I went for some walks on my own. He cried when I left, as though he understood that I was going away and wondered whether I would come back. Although of course he was too little to think that, to comprehend.

Once I went out of the house, down the stairs, continued down the street and on to the city center. I found a cinema, bought a ticket and watched the movie that started half an hour later. When I returned the house was silent. I thought that he perhaps was sleeping, but when he fell asleep after crying, his nose was always blocked, and he usually made a noise, a snoring sound. I did not hear anything like that now. It was completely silent. I remember that I stepped across the floor and over to the cot, that it took some time to reach the bed.

When I peered in, he lay looking back at me, blinked, as though he had been lying waiting and had decided to be patient. He followed me with his gaze as I walked around the cot. And then he closed his eyes.

A CHILDREN'S NURSE I spoke to. She helped me to find out where I had to go, what papers I had to sign. She said nothing. She had come across women like me before, I don't believe I was the only one who gave her son away. He was six months old when I gave him up. He wore a knitted jacket and cap. I sat with him on my knee in a tiny office. Outside there was grass and a garden. I had seen that when I arrived. A little garden outside the house. When I lifted him out of the baby carriage, naturally he started to cry. But inside the office he stopped, he kept his eyes on me when they carried him out. And with that he was gone.

They said I could have an address, but I did not want that. I was so relieved when I got rid of him. Those round cheeks, those arms that clutched at the air. All that crying. Years went by before I thought of him again, or allowed myself to think about him. It was an unfortunate relationship, the only thing I felt was relief.

But later I thought about him, I wondered perhaps where he was, who was looking after him. Whether they were treating him better than I had.

THE APPLICATION FORM has no address, nothing to indicate where it should go, who it is intended for. It can be sent or not sent. I don't know where I should go with it or hand it in. Helena will probably tell me what to do. The smooth sheet is placed between the papers. I have started to fill it out, I have put it down again. It makes me feel slightly numb, nauseous, I always feel that I need to go to the toilet when I take it out. Nervousness makes me need to go to the toilet.

At night sometimes I awaken with a sense of unease, not fear or anxiety. It is perhaps the episode with the intruder I am thinking about, it is so old now, it is an unease I cannot explain. I pad through the house, check the lights, tidy away a newspaper on the table, a cup left behind in the living room, food Simon has left lying on a plate, things like that. I enter the kitchen and check that the burners are switched off, the coffee percolator, that everything is as it should be, I look around. Sometimes I drink a glass of water, switching off the light and returning to bed where I most often fall into a deep sleep, as you do when you are far too tired. But one night not so long ago I remained standing in the living room looking out the window, out into the garden, as I often do, but not at that time of night, and everything was truly different, it was so early in the morning. The light bluish, as though the darkness was just being diluted, gradually replaced by more and more radiance, only the silhouettes remained without being washed out. I stood looking at the garden that now had such an unfamiliar character. The houses on the other side, several up on the hillside, the regulation distance. We know very few of them, even though we live so close, although we have spent all these years here; the young couple in the neighboring property, another couple just beside us, they have recently retired I believe, the guy with the young cleaner. I wonder what they say about us. While I stood there, I began to think about Simon, whether he missed having someone to confide in. I thought about his wish for me to look for my son. Again that thought pops up, that underneath everything, the house, the children, all the years of movement and unrest, there has been, this silence. That it has simply risen to the surface, pushed up by external changes. Like a splinter of stone is forced up by the innards of the earth, by disturbances in the soil, and gradually comes to light in the spring. And that is what really frightens me. How it reminds me of something else. Is it meaninglessness?

ANOTHER NIGHT I dreamed that Simon was what he has always been, that he came and sat down on the edge of the bed, in fact I thought I had just awoken from a dream, and he had coffee and newspapers with him and one of those scones Marija sometimes baked and put in the freezer, and that make me believe that she is still here, that she is standing out in the kitchen or some other place in the house busy with something, and I was happy about it and at the same time that Simon was eating again, and Simon was talking incessantly, it was obviously an important conversation, or: What he said was important, but when I tried to understand what it was, the words seemed disconnected, I could not manage to put them together into meaningful sentences.

When I awoke, really awoke, he was lying beside me.

I could take his hand, stroke his freckled hands, his gray hair. But I couldn't manage to do that. I can't manage to accept it. I had an urge to say, pull yourself together, say something. This is not you. Be who you are, the person I recognize, now I am tired of this.

But I didn't do that. I had also become silent. I got up, and when I turned around he was lying there watching me from the bed, and his expression was clear and present, I wondered whether it was lust I saw in his eyes. I was taken aback. I pulled on my dressing gown and left the room.

NOT SO LONG ago I woke and saw that a wasp had come into the bedroom. Simon has developed an allergy to wasps, or perhaps he has always had it, in theory a sting could kill him. The window was open, it must have come in that way, managing to force its way through the flimsy curtain covering the opening, perhaps only a few minutes earlier, or it could have circled around the room for a while, maybe it had not woken me until it approached the bed. It seemed confused, it was making a noise that was low and intense.

He was sleeping, I noticed that the wasp was moving along the exposed part of his forearm, he was sleeping on his side with one hand under his cheek and the other naked arm across his head, as though trying to protect it. He often sleeps like that. It was early morning. I slept deeply and must have awoken gradually although I felt I had awoken abruptly, and only a few inches in front of me, I saw the movement. I remained lying completely still and watched. Close up it was large, even when I looked at it compared to his arm, his hand. Simon's skin, pale with freckles over the back of his hand. The wasp remained motionless on his skin, lifting and lowering its wings.

Both equally helpless, the wasp that probably had no harmful intention, and Simon's bare arm that he was unable to pull away in his sleep, the danger he could not see. They were left to their own devices.

I was the only one who could do something.

If he had been awake, he would have lain completely still, stiff, while we both would have expected me to get rid of the insect.

I stared at it, now it flew to the skin beside his temple.

After a spell it took off, circled the bed, resting somewhere on the white bedside table, and so on around the room, I got up, found a newspaper and chased it toward the open window. When I lay down in bed again, Simon had wakened, he looked at me, in the same way as I had looked at the wasp, without making any move.

He said: Did you get it out?

I got it out, I said, surprised to hear his voice.

Thanks, he said.

I remember I remained lying there looking at the ceiling, with him lying silently at my side. He did not say anything more.

We were to celebrate our wedding anniversary. It was only a few weeks after the dismissal, and after Marija had left. A red-letter day. Simon and I did not say anything about the fact that she had been looking forward to it, that we had discussed and planned the celebration with her as well. We talked about a family party, perhaps a trip, we had invited the girls, we wanted to mark the day with a gathering. We spent the days picturing the party in our minds, it gave us something to do, to look forward to.

I had risen early on the day and set the long table in the living room, we were planning to have much of the party outside in the garden, but the weather looked uncertain. Nevertheless Simon labored at hanging up lanterns in the trees. We had not attempted that before. He had an idea that the lanterns would give a lovely illumination when darkness fell.

I had received a phone call from Helena, she was not feeling too well, I told her to take it easy, she sounded so unhappy, I thought there was perhaps something more to it, something at work, or with her boyfriend. But she brushed it aside. She was exhausted, she said. I should have asked her why she was exhausted, perhaps she would have told me then, warned me. Would it have spared Simon, us. Would it have made things any different?

I see us going around in the house that morning, we take out the beautiful brass candlesticks, hold the tablecloth above the table, him at one end, me at the other, it hovers like a sail and lands on the tabletop. He fetches plates and cutlery, polishes the candlesticks one more time as well as the little dessert spoons.

They are expected around four o'clock, we have plenty of time, we do everything slowly, carefully so as not to use up the tasks too quickly, there is still a while before they are to arrive. Besides, these very tasks hold a particular pleasure that should not be denied, this sense of anticipation because we are already familiar with these occasions, we know all about the good, gratifying pattern they normally follow.

The girls and their husbands. The children running in and out of the veranda door, between the table with soft drinks and goodies and back to the garden, red in the face and perspiring, absorbed in the game outdoors. The teenagers meeting up on the little raised platform, gawky in their stiff clothes, envious of the children for a while before hitting upon their own version or perversion of the game with the children as lowly servants. The husbands, uncomfortable until they have had a beer, gather under the eaves on the terrace, their trouser legs pulled up, their jackets over the chair arms now that there is heat in the air, it will probably be a warm afternoon and evening. Simon is talking to them, he likes that sense of contact, although none of them has an occupation similar to his. They are IT professionals, and one is a teacher.

It has happened so many times. That's the way it usually goes. Later I think about it, I know how it should have progressed, how the party should have been.

They were to arrive about four o'clock. And so the tablecloth lands on the table, the candlesticks are shining much too brightly, Simon calls out to me twice, I think they're coming now, he means he can hear the cars parking up in the street. The living room is transformed, or reemerges as the living room in which similar parties have been held previously, the living room that can be viewed in photographs we have taken during festivities like this, but that disappears between family parties and is handed over to the daily round once more. It is so obvious that the children used to ask about it even when they were small, then it was their birthdays we were celebrating, an odd time we had a visit from couples, friends of ours: There is another living room inside the living room. The little ones wondered where it went when we were alone.

We think we hear cars continually, we stop and listen. But the voices, the footsteps on the driveway remain outside.

THE DOORBELL RANG. We looked at each other, and he stood up in his newly purchased suit. I saw what he was thinking: at last.

Now they are here, I said. I stepped quietly toward the door, I did not want to do anything different from how it usually went. Even the act of opening the door was part of the joy of the whole thing.

A neighbor was standing outside. I could have seen her face through the glass of the narrow alcove window at the side of the door if I hadn't been so preoccupied with opening the door quickly, I was so sure that I already had them on my retina, the girls, their husbands, their families. She explained something about a community project among several neighbors. And as she stood before me, without excusing herself or asking if she was disturbing us, my only thought was why don't you go away. I was not listening. I was so taken aback. Simon still stood on the same spot when I returned to the living room.

No, was all I said. As though to a question that had not been asked.

Oh well, he said.

I went into the kitchen and placed plastic wrap over the sandwiches. I pulled out the plug from the percolator, it seemed as though the action was important, logical and right. I remained standing looking at the calendar. I closed my eyes.

I may have stood there for a while. What are you doing? he said. I turned around, and he was standing in the doorway.

Do you think they're coming? he said.

Of course they're coming, I said to him.

Yes, he said.

We sat down in the living room, outside the light was fading, as it does on summer evenings when darkness does not fall abruptly, but gradually. I put on a CD, the music drifted through the rooms. It enveloped us. But at some point, he walked over and turned it down, even though the volume was already so low that it could not possibly have drowned out the doorbell.

I couldn't say a word. I looked at him, he smiled. A troubled smile that was insistent and said *they'll probably be here soon.*

We tried to phone them, but no one answered. We continued this performance. I think neither of us knew how to conclude it. Restless actors who have reached a point in the play and there are no instructions or possibilities for further improvisation, and all that remains is to decide how to bring it to a close. He straightened a plate, placed a fresh candle in one of the candlesticks, it struck me that we had forgotten to set out napkins.

We circled around the conspicuous emptiness. I picked up a book, pretending to read. I knew I had to say something, I didn't have the strength.

He walked across the floor, turned and again came to a halt.

Eva, he said, I don't think—

Before he reached the end of his sentence, we heard the doorbell. We looked at each other.

HE WAS THE one who went to open the door.

They came in together. He and Helena. She was wearing a flimsy dress with long sleeves. She came over to me and gave me a hug.

We sat inside, although it was a warm evening, the lanterns outside the window, the ones he had placed at the bottom of the garden and planned to light at dusk.

I want to say something, she said.

But she didn't say anything immediately. The music was still playing, softly and floating on the brink of being inaudible.

We ate and perhaps tried to find a reason to avoid saying anything. We all knew what it was about. The irritation that had built up, the girls were in a way punishing us, for something they could not fathom.

Helena put it into words, although we already knew by then. That their anger was connected with their irritation over Marija's dismissal, and it had led to other annoyances coming to the surface. Now they had decided, all of them, to stay at home. Punish us. She did not say that, but I suspected it was so. I don't understand it, she said after a while, none of us understands it, but I accept it. If you could only give a better explanation. Especially for Kirsten and Greta. Explain to them what it's all about.

She had brought a gift with her, a vase, she flattened and smoothed out the wrapping paper, folding the corners carefully, layer upon layer. And now it was a square in her hands. They think we are stubborn, Simon said, smiling and stroking Helena on the cheek.

Mom, Helena said, turning to me.

But there is nothing to be said, I replied.

She looked at me, she was so disappointed.

SHE LEFT AFTER a couple of hours, we ate some of the chicken wings, Helena did most of the talking. Simon did not say so much. We held the wings between our fingers, I had never liked holding on to bones while I was eating. I ate only a few. Helena was telling us something, I can no longer remember what, I don't even know if I was listening. Afterward she helped me to tidy up. We put the rest of the food into the fridge, I filled the kitchen sink with water, outside the light was tinged with red as though it had really been the day we had hoped for and now it was over, I leaned across the sink.

Helena hugged me before she left. She always does that.

It is unfair, I thought, but also our own fault.

I COULD PHONE them, say that I thought it was unfair, but in a way they had a right, I thought, to such anger. After all we had held back from them throughout the years, not only about Marija, but all the other things too. As though we had been lying.

It was never the intention, I would say, we only thought it was for the best. For everyone. He would avoid going through it again, the sadness, the depression. There are things we cannot understand, I felt.

And me? Perhaps I was cowardly.

I have understood that I have been wrong, I would say. But would that help? It was all a mean, contemptible little protest, I thought. We cleared the table while we walked around the house, in the silence.

I so wanted to say something, ease some of the pain. I said that he didn't need to do it all now, some things could wait till the next day. I know that, he replied. His hands were shaking, he cleared away the dinner service. In order to avoid waking up and finding it there, a confirmation of the disappointment.

I saw him that evening, going around the garden taking down the colorful lanterns one by one. I remember it crossing my mind that now we'll never see how they shine.

THEY PHONED LATER and said that there had been a misunderstanding, pleaded an excuse. What did they blame it on? I don't remember. We knew that they were lying, and of course they knew it too. I believe they regretted it, of course they did, it was a rotten thing to do. We accepted their excuses and had some kind of celebration a short time afterward, but it was not as we had planned, it was not our big day. We knew, and they knew.

HE WANTED TO tell them about it. He said it was time the girls got to know. During the following days he prepared himself, made himself ready to talk about what we have not managed to say during all these years, I believe he was searching for the right moment. Will it change anything, I recall thinking. Will they not simply become even angrier, because we haven't said anything before? He could not stop talking about it. It was as though he were ready to spring, over and over again. I was the one he talked to, I heard about the people who surrounded him when he was a child, women, men, families, names that are forgotten.

One night he woke and told me he could see the apartment he had lived in as a child, before the war, before the Germans occupied his hometown. He was able to go inside it. Even in his thoughts he opened the door gingerly, in case anything was waiting inside for him that he had not anticipated, he stepped inside, he said, evidently after everyone had departed. The long curtains that reach the floor in front of each of the living room windows, he has a glimpse of the kitchen, glasses and plates are washed and sitting on the kitchen counter, with the towel draped over them. In this illusion, this memory, he sees himself open the closet in the hallway, smells the familiar odor of them, but his parents' clothes are not there. He goes around and catches sight of his brother's shoes, his own. He continues into the foyer. It feels as though they are present and at the same time he realizes that they are not. In the living room he remains standing in a particular spot where he remembers standing when he was little, a spot that gave him a kind of overview of what the others were doing, his parents who used to walk to and fro through the rooms, occupied with various tasks.

There is sunshine outside the window, he said, but the ocher-colored woven curtains are drawn, rather than the blackout blinds. Except for one window, where the black blind is pulled down as though it is a wall, a fireplace wall.

He also catches sight of something else.

Simon is thinking about his young aunt and cousin, the two who stayed on, waiting for the boy's father and for the helpers who were to take them to him.

That is what he sees; sometimes when he believes he is in this apartment, he notices something lying on a counter, he picks it up and it is a pair of glasses, the frame is strengthened around the thick lenses, but the glasses themselves are not large. One of the little screws is slightly loose, he lifts them up, the gentle curve at the end of the leg, the hoop that attaches behind the ear, beneath the hair. He clutches the glasses, they smell of something he recognizes, earwax. There is in fact a certain smell of earwax, he notices it, he imagines he smells it, now there is no difference between the two things. He thinks he remembers his cousin used to put them down when he washed himself, that he has seen them there before. He discovers the washing water sitting undisturbed in a bowl, a bluish film on top, the remains of the soap. And he understands that they were picked up suddenly, forced out, his cousin who can't see properly, who has this visual impairment, everything is just a fog without his glasses, they would not have left without his glasses if there was time, and that's the way he knows, he tells me, knows that they were chased out, and his cousin who probably can't distinguish anything other than hazy colors and light, figures merging together and dividing up again. And perhaps, he says, it is just as well.

SIMON RELATED THAT he had heard his parents talking just before they all went into hiding. They were standing in the hallway in the old apartment and holding a conversation. They were talking about their father having contacted his former employer in an attempt to obtain assistance. He had worked in an office for as long as it was possible for people like him to do so. The old boss had said to Simon's father that he had nothing against helping them, he just could not understand how it could be done. Whether it would really make any difference to their situation. Simon's father had explained to him that it might perhaps postpone things. But, his boss had said as he looked at him with a worried face, do you not consider that the police have a reason for doing what they are doing. I didn't know what to say, Simon's father said to his wife as they stood in the hallway with Simon listening from the children's bedroom. He was my boss.

His boss had also pointed out that it would not be good for the reputation of the business. It would undoubtedly place them all in a negative light if it came out that they had tried to do something against the wishes of the authorities. Everything he said had been sensible in the circumstances, there were of course several ways to look at it. And his father had said he agreed, he had nodded. Because he did not dare to do anything else, because he was used to refraining from contradicting his boss. He had said that he understood.

While we stood there talking, Simon's father said to his wife out there in the hallway, the weather had cleared up. Outside the building in which the office was situated, the sky had come into view. We could see toward the city, and it was a fine day.

He took my hand and wished me good luck, his father said. I know you will make the best of the situation, he said. And what did you say, Simon's mother asked. I said yes and returned his handshake, Simon heard his father say.

She took my father's hat, said Simon, opened the closet in the hallway and hung his overcoat inside next to our clothes. I can still smell the scent of that closet, of old shoes, worn-out soles, the shoe polish she had hidden. His coat. Our clothes beside it. They waited in the hallway for a moment after that. I don't know what they were doing. Perhaps they just stood still. In their apartment, outside the clothes closet. She who had just hung up his coat, he by her side. Just stood there, before they came in to us children.

•

HE ALSO RECALLED another event immediately before they went into hiding. He had been with his mother to one of the places where it was still possible for his family to shop, and she had not had enough money to pay, perhaps because the prices, the cost of the commodities, appeared to vary and increase every time they were there, she had acted as though it were a common occurrence, and asked him to run home to fetch another purse. And he had sprinted, and when he returned, his mother was standing in a line among several people about to be arrested.

He approached her, perhaps to associate himself with her or at least to give her the money. She had not met his eye, but let her gaze slide as indifferently over him as she let it slide over the other spectators, he halted and moved backward. Simon remained standing among the spectators while she was forced up onto a truck, and not once did she look at him as though they knew each other.

She had come back again, amazingly enough she had not been held for long. But for several days he regarded her in a different light, as though they actually were unknown to each other. He thought about who she really was. He remembered the stories she had told him and that he had only sometimes listened to, about when she met his father, about when they were young. He suddenly understood that she was an individual separate from him. He looked at her clothes in the wardrobe, he observed how she put her hair up, holding the hairpins in her mouth while she attached them, put on her coat and hat to go out, stroked her hand over her ankle when she came home, because the shoes she had acquired were too tight, he tried to discover who she was, view her from outside. When he looked at her name enough times in succession, it seemed strange, disconcerting. He saw her as she had always been, but it seemed as though that was not enough. It was like looking at a picture sketched so that the contours showed a figure, but if you looked at it for long enough, it also formed the outline of a different figure. He saw that now, with her. And it was a more fundamental change than everything that was happening around them, in the midst of the upheavals he caught sight of her. It both terrified and delighted him.

WHEN THEY WENT into hiding, there were several people involved in concealing them, he especially remembered a woman from a religious community. Her strictness. Simon thought he recalled that she was the sister of the woman who had taken him along to church. The mood of these people would be changeable, their motives varied, there could be days they doubted, it was not so easy to understand why they all became helpers, perhaps it was by chance, perhaps they had a guilty conscience, perhaps their religion or some other conviction decreed it, regardless: Their approach varied. His parents always spoke carefully in low voices to these men and women, and gradually it dawned on him how dependent they were on them, how none of them would have been alive without the helpers who could also be called guards, and that they could anytime at all change their minds and disappear. It was the food the helpers brought that kept them alive, him and his family, their dependency made the captives helpless, Simon understood that, and how it was reflected in his parents' expressions, how they talked to that woman who was frequently impatient and bad tempered, and whom they nevertheless never dared to contradict or confront despite her occasional unreasonableness. He recalled that his mother had broken down one evening after the woman had left, sobbing and saying that she could not stand it any longer.

Even power, the need to control that perhaps first came to light through this new influence over others, or perhaps it had always been there. That was part of the reason why the woman, and maybe several of the others as well, had gone along with helping them in the first place. None of us knew their genuine motives, Simon said.

HE TOLD ME again about his upbringing, the hiding place, eventually repeating many of the details, as though by repeating them, he held them tight. He described how everything in their hiding place had a stale taste of dust, even the air tasted of dust, the limited food they ate, the lukewarm water they drank, it is dust he thinks of first and foremost when he is trying to describe it.

He told me things he had never mentioned before, perhaps he had not remembered them earlier. It was exactly as if he had gained access to another room, he went inside, came out again, went in and out between the past and the present. But finally it seemed as though he could not get through, something was closed, the openness gradually passed, he shut himself inside. I had thought he wanted to tell the girls, but now he no longer wanted to talk about it. And one morning when I came into the living room, he was sitting in his chair with a blanket covering him, he must have risen during the night. He was sitting still with the blanket over his shoulders, with an expression, a grimace that I found disturbing. I became afraid, I shook him gently. He opened his eyes and looked at me. But he said nothing.

It did not pass. When the children were little, they played a game in which they made a pact not to speak, it was all about who could hold out the longest. Only the one magic word from any of them could break the pact.

I didn't possess that word.

And there we were, going around in the house, and there were times, I thought, that it appeared he was simply waiting for me to come out with something, an answer. As though the silence was a challenge rather than an absence of words.

SIMON AND HIS closest family were taken to a different place during the night, a new hiding place where they stayed until the war was over, they all survived. But their relatives, their friends, their life outside had vanished. His parents were changed after the war, Simon said. They just became older, they always seemed small when he visited them in the rooms of their new apartment. The transition to his own adult life, when he visited his parents less often, coincided with their transition to these other rooms, in their new apartment, that in comparison with the hiding place seemed gigantic, and made its inhabitants tiny. They were submerged, becoming extinguished by the massive walls, the enormous high-ceilinged rooms of the apartment where they lived, as though by solemnity. Passed away long before our own children were born. He did not manage to maintain contact with the brother who had shared the silence during all the time they spent in their hiding place. Their conversations were always short and hesitant. As though they could not let go of the only thing that had saved them, the silence. Their contact is erased, it takes only a few years.

He still received letters from his second cousin, Irit Meyer. She also forwarded letters from the organization that was searching for further information about those who disappeared during the Holocaust. The little round second cousin, or his "dear cousin" as he liked to call her, who was no longer so plump, but stayed in a nursing home in Schöneberg in Berlin, she sent a picture of herself, and she was surrounded by all the things I remembered from her little apartment, probably all the furniture was simply crammed together in a smaller area, and in the midst of it all she sat with the same exuberant hairstyle as in the prewar photographs. By her side there was a man smiling oddly as though he were pulling down his top lip at the same time as he tried to push up his bottom lip and the corners. Ralph and I, she wrote. But she wrote nothing about who this Ralph was, I assumed that he was another resident. Although she had moved to the nursing home, she wrote her own little letters about her existence down there. Letters that I opened and handed to him right up until they stopped coming sometime last year, and I haven't had the strength to find out why, in order to avoid telling Simon about yet another person who has gone.

His cousin. His cousin was missing. He was this child nobody found. Simon searched for years for information about him. Where he was killed, precisely what had happened. Only recently something has turned up, it has taken a long time to find out.

Before the silence it was this cousin who preoccupied Simon, this young cousin, perhaps also his aunt. He would not rest, he insisted, not until he knew what had happened to them, a sentence he had from one of Irit's letters, she had at least written something similar. Previously he replied to all her letters, and she forwarded the odd letter from this organization. Her letters enclosed photographs copied onto glossy, flimsy photo paper. Their kin. People who, when I look at these pictures of them, manifest themselves as illustrations in a book, none of them resembling him. They are vaguely obscure, shuttered and restricted within the photographs like memorial plaques from which no one can any longer tear them.

HE NEVER TOLD them about it, although he planned and practiced all these evenings, nights, days, when he went over the painful aspects of the past with me. Instead he became more and more silent. As though the recollection of the past, of these events, had been only the start of an interior journey, backward, as though the memories he had initially considered so vivid, changed, he said they were no longer so easy to access, complained that he felt as though he were standing outside them looking in, they became untouchable, tableaux on display in glass cases, they were something he could not catch hold of. And therefore could no longer attempt to explain. In the end he chose silence. Was that how it was?

I think I see him standing leaning over the newspaper that is placed on the table, he often looks at the newspaper pages as though he is studying one of his maps, leafing restlessly through, putting it away, taking it up again, as though he has to check once more that the overview he has gained, the impression of changes and movements within this unstable atlas, still holds good. Now he is bent over the newspaper, if I ask him what he wants for dinner, he will shrug his shoulders and smile. It's up to me.

I look at his hand again. He turns the page of the newspaper. I go across to him, he looks up in surprise, perhaps I place my hand over his on the table. We remain like this for several minutes.

I AWOKE ONE night after the unfortunate wedding anniversary, it was about seven or eight weeks later, and he was not there. He had left the bed and gone into the living room.

When I came in he was sitting in the semidarkness.

Simon, I said, I could hear the uncertainty in my own voice, I am anxious. I do not like him sitting up during the night.

It is two months ago now, he said. He meant Marija. Her dismissal. Two months since she had left us. Yes, I answered. It will be that.

I believe it was.

He stopped, waited.

I think it was impossible to know.

Yes, I said.

He just sat. He had a glass of cognac in front of him. He seldom drank late in the evening.

We could have loaned her money, he said.

Why should we have done that, I had an urge to say.

Yes, I said. Paid our way out of it, I thought without saying it aloud. As though we had actually done something wrong. As though it had been us.

But it's not too late, he said. We could perhaps get in touch with her. Tomorrow. Perhaps give her a small loan all the same.

I hesitated with my reply, he nursed his glass carefully.

Yes, we could do that right enough, I said.

He stood up, his movement showed signs of him having sat there for a long time, stiffness in his back. He stepped over to the window, looking out at the garden. I knew he dreamed often, that he still had nightmares.

I too went over to the window. I was thinking about my brother, he said. It's a long time since I have thought of him.

I nodded. Outside, a bird flew low over the lawn in the darkness. He peered after it too. I saw that he was old, it was quite obvious now, I noticed it in the same way you might notice that someone has become soaked in the rain or has forgotten to fasten some buttons on a shirt. It feels of similarly transitory importance when I note it in him. Although it's not like that. And I thought: I must appreciate that it isn't transitory. He is not going to be able to shrug off old age.

We could invite some old colleagues, he said.

Yes, I replied.

It would be nice to meet someone.

We ought to go to bed soon, I said.

He finished his cognac, placing the empty glass on the windowsill.

What were you thinking about your brother, I said.

He looked at me, said that it was hazy, everything had happened while he was half asleep.

I have forgotten to switch off the light, he added. The light is still on in the garage.

He released his breath, waited, and in the ensuing silence that drew all attention toward itself, he remained standing there with his hand halfway over his mouth. Let's go to bed, he said.

HE HAS NEVER made any attempt to find his brother in recent years. If he knew where his brother was, I don't know whether he would look him up. I even mentioned it once, that he hadn't really taken care of his brother. His brother existed somewhere, in an apartment, in a town, even though a long time had passed. His brother who walked about and remembered and knew, and could have talked about it. In contrast to those who were gone.

He came here once. The brother. One single time, while the girls were so small that they don't remember him. A slightly built, serious man, he did not look like Simon, he smoked a great deal, drank rather excessively, they conversed in the language that Simon never used at other times, something that made Greta laugh, she was only a few years old, but she laughed whenever that man opened his mouth. At first I believe it confused him, but then he permitted her to approach him, allowed her to take his hand and sit on his knee. Greta continued to laugh every time someone spoke in this foreign language. She touched his mouth, made him open it wide, he was patient, she touched his lips, his teeth, as though she wanted to look and see if the strange words were inside there, if that was where they came from or if they were somewhere else altogether.

He was a nervous, slightly drunken man. He stayed with us for a few days, he was to stay for a whole week, but I believe they ran out of things to talk about, he and Simon. And he had to return home. There was something he had to go home for, something vague. I saw that they sat in their own chairs without talking to each other. They could perhaps cope with their own silence, but not the other's, and they never sat or stood close to each other. I thought that they *could* no longer be close, that the physical closeness that was forced upon them during the war meant that they could not bear to be too close to each other, just the smell, the voice, the body and the feeling of the other person there must be enough to remind them, perhaps even give them the feeling of being back, shut inside. They sat in their individual chairs, their separation by mutual agreement, I thought, as if they both agreed to keep their distance, now that they had finally acquired the personal space they must have dreamed of when they shared a bed and kept themselves occupied in the hiding place, now that they were at last set free from closeness, that closed in, desperate symbiosis.

Not until the airport. After Simon's brother had taken out his ticket for the journey home, after we had said bon voyage and he was about to board, they both took a step forward, suddenly hugged each other, embracing with a tight grip, and not unlike the beginning of a fight, held each other fiercely as I imagined two wrestlers might perhaps do, only closer, really inseparable, they merged into one, two wrestlers checking out each other's strength before throwing themselves onto the ground and one of them gains the upper hand. They let go again. Neither of them wept, neither of them looked as upset or moved as that moment of intimacy would suggest. The brother walked toward the airplane, and Simon was left behind. Only Greta took a few steps after him, as though she wanted to accompany the uncle she had come to know slightly, unwilling to give him up just like that. She looked questioningly at us and at the exit to the runway. But Simon simply said: Now we'll go home.

HIS BROTHER TOLD us something while he was here. It seemed as though he was putting down a heavy burden and then journeyed on. He had heard their parents talk about it, he said. Before they left their apartment during the war, they said nothing to their neighbors on that stairway. Nothing about where they were going or why. There was no one who could be trusted, or else it was impossible to know whom you might be able to trust. Every day the neighbors walked past the locked door, and there was little cause for curiosity. The family had left, the door was locked, the windows in darkness. One of the neighbors had a dog, what was it called, oh yes, Kaiser. And that dog usually stopped outside the door, barking, sat down and barked as if it were waiting for something. Waiting for someone to open up, a stupid dog. The owner of course tried to drag it off with him, it protested loudly, as was stated later. The neighbor scolded, threatened. But the dog was insistent. It would not desist. As though it had caught the scent of something inside.

The same performance was repeated every day. The dog sat down. Barked. Pawed as though it were possible to burrow underneath the doormat, under the threshold, the doorframe. But the apartment is definitely empty, people said. The occupants left ages ago, the boy who knew the dog and took it for walks has left with his family. He won't be coming out no matter how much the dog barks. The neighbor speaks sternly to the animal, he almost has to deliver a kick, to the dog, in order to get it to come with him. The next day the same procedure. The day after. Until the dog owner and another neighbor have a chat. It is the other one who has become suspicious. Has someone broken in, entered the empty rooms, inside the apartment? It is possible of course. It is dark, it is silent there, but it is possible all the same.

He notifies the police.

HE NOTIFIED THE police, Simon's brother told Simon. The police arrive, they knock on the door, shout. It is silent inside. The apartment is empty, a neighbor says, thrusting his head out from another doorway on the same landing. The family has left. It's only that daft dog. The boy who lived there before has spoiled it, taught it to receive a reward when it sits outside there and barks. That's why it does it. Barks as if it's calling for him. Disturbs the whole block. But the boy is long gone, like the family, no one knows what's become of them. Another one gets involved, but it is obvious the dog has got wind of something, he says. Look at it. As if it is sitting there waiting for its master. You would think it was the boy's dog. The police shout a warning again, eventually breaking down the locked door. The neighbors crowd around their windows. And after only a few minutes they emerge. The dog was right. The apartment is not empty. There is a woman there, a child.

They are picked up that morning, taken away. The neighbors watch them drive off in a car. A woman and a child aged five or six. The hound was not stupid.

It never ends, all this about the dog.

Simon exonerates the dog, but not himself.

He sat up more often in the evenings talking about the events of the war. It made me uneasy. And so, after all the repetitions, the ruminations put into words, the interpretations of everything that had happened, the time in the hiding place and prior to that, it was as though he started to run empty, as though he exhausted himself. He spoke less and more rarely. And eventually he spoke more rarely about other things as well, to me, to others.

Until he stopped saying more than what was routine. Good day. Hello.

Now that I am not admitted, I simply long for him to talk, anything at all, I would listen.

We are alone together when it is quiet.

He said that he liked the silence so much after we had moved here, out of the center, that he liked how still and bright it was. That is a long time ago now.

I often lie awake listening to the susurration of the trees, the rain in summertime, falling on the planks of the terrace floor, the garage roof. Soundlessness in the rooms and outside.

Not so long ago I saw an advertisement, animals for sale. Puppies at a kennel. There were pictures of them, they were lying curled together on newspaper with large heads and ruffled pelts. I studied the picture, I liked the tiniest one that had clearly ended up slightly outside the rest of the litter, so I cut out the phone number, it is still hanging on the refrigerator. I have seen dogs when I walk about in the neighborhood here. I have thought a little about getting a new dog. We could have gone for walks, the dog and I. It could probably make contact with Simon, perhaps it would have done him good. There are dogs that can be trained to communicate with their owners, they understand. He would not need to speak to it. Dogs are intuitive, where have I heard that. Loyal to their master.

A new dog could guard the house as well.

She did not like dogs, Marija, but when I reflect on it, I can't recall that she ever gave a good reason for why she felt that way, that she ever explained it in a rational fashion, or in a fashion I could understand. It was not true that she was afraid of them.

She just did not like them.

Marija's daughter managed to throw her man out, was it in May during the spring that she came running to tell me that? Marija had phoned her every single day, and in the middle of her work she would have to answer her phone, something she never did otherwise. We appreciated that it was important, we heard her walking to and fro out in the hallway, we could not of course understand what she was saying. But we could make out our own names. Afterward she came through to the kitchen and told us that some important things were going to take place now.

We invited her to dinner. First she cleaned the house, helped out in the kitchen and afterward sat down in the dining room as though she had just come in the door, she had changed her clothes, she had a different smell. She must have dabbed on perfume, it was slightly unfamiliar, later I associated the evening with the scent of that perfume, a distinctive odor of chrysanthemums. But perhaps she had also used it before, she used it on special occasions such as when she was looking forward to something.

Sit down and eat, I said.

I really should have prepared the food, she said. But I told her that it was not necessary, I had already roasted the meat and boiled the potatoes and broccoli, and while we were eating, her phone rang. We heard her speaking in this language that I actually cannot recall ever hearing before Marija came here. Now it has happened, she shouted and began to tell us about it while she was still standing out in the hallway. She has left him. And best of all: She's coming, Marija said, with the phone in her hand. At last she's coming!

Her daughter was to arrive the following Sunday, together with Marija's brother. They were both going to stay at Marija's house, and although I offered them accommodation at our house, Marija turned that down for quite a while. She was unwilling. I said that I would not give in. Then she yielded reluctantly. They would not be any bother, she said.

I was not looking forward to it, I was happy about her excitement, but it is true, I was not happy about having strangers in the house.

The uncle, Marija's brother, was a man with thinning hair and an outbreak of rosacea spreading a blush across his face and giving him an agitated appearance, he was also unusually tall, like having a giant come to visit, a giant who went around the house and never seemed able to find a chair to fit. In any case he seldom sat down. When he spoke his voice contrasted starkly with his appearance, soft and high pitched. He offered to repair an old refrigerator we have in the garage, but on Marija's advice we refused the offer, he cannot repair anything, she said, he works at the cash desk in a gas station, he is just trying to be useful. Marija had told us that her daughter was totally different from her, and that was true. She seemed shy and depressed, she was small, slim and had a little girl with her who continually sat on her lap. The uncle smoked with the terrace doors slightly ajar, something that led to a constant draft during those days. The girl, the child, was called something beginning with *B*, a name I learned to pronounce, but that I have forgotten now.

Marija prepared the meals, several every day, and I discovered that I enjoyed the company. Even the girl who sat up late in the evenings until she fell asleep on her mother's knee and was carried up to bed. The uncle was simply present, he sat still for a few minutes at a time, before obviously feeling the need to move again, to try out a new chair, a different position while he peered in the direction of the garage door and the broken lamp on the outdoor light. He asked several times whether he could fix something. We went on an outing to the aquarium at Nordnes. B had a special way of showing eagerness, instead of smiling or shouting like the other children who were there, she clenched her fists, tightening her jaw, as though her excitement was almost unbearable. Especially when one of the employees came to feed the penguins, she tensed up in that way, almost like a temporary spasticity.

Marija was concerned about her, I saw that she kept her eye on the girl. The child had experienced problems at school, Marija explained, she had become a scapegoat, for no reason whatsoever, these things of course happen for no reason at all, she said. She did not know what she should do. Take her out, find another school, when she talked about it, the daughter did not want to listen, she already had too many worries about her job and her former boyfriend. Marija held her granddaughter's hand and bought her whatever she wanted, a book of fairy tales, a soft toy animal, in the evening she read the girl a fairy story, a Norwegian edition of *Grimms' Fairy Tales*, she read the Norwegian text and translated it.

Who is it that took the children away with him? The Pied Piper of Hamelin, he played his pipe and lured all the rats to follow him in a long line down to the river where they drowned. When he returned to Hamelin, they did not think they needed to keep their promise to him. They would not pay him.

She read everything on the page, did not skip over anything. She conjured it up, and the girl tensed her jaw.

When he began to play again, it was not the rats that followed the Pied Piper through the town's narrow streets, but all the boys and girls, all the children of Hamelin. They came out from the schools, from the houses.

I observed Marija and her granddaughter as Marija read the distressing story to the little girl who sat there with her eyes full of terror. While I listened, I suddenly felt unwell, perhaps it was something to do with the ghastly story. Simon had already gone to bed. He was lying in bed with the light on, I put my arm around him, and he put his arm around me. I think we both lay listening to the voices, the foreign language. People we barely knew, who were occupying our living room.

The Pied Piper has a pipe, and the children follow him. They follow him in a long line, he leads them out of Hamelin, toward a mountain. He plays his pipe louder, an opening appears. Right into the mountainside, into a cavern, he leads them inside. And there they vanish.

AFTER THEY HAD left, she was brokenhearted. She spoke to her daughter on her phone again, the daughter's unpleasant boyfriend had returned. Marija said there was nothing she could do for her, for the young girl. She was discouraged about being so far away, but she felt that it would not have been any different if she had visited them. She would not listen, she said about her daughter. We talked about our daughters, how it was impossible to control other people's lives, but instead we had to sit and watch things happen.

That was when I suggested that she continue to live here with us for a while, in the meantime at least. She had problems where she was living, an increase in rent that meant she had to look for another place all the same. You can stay with us, we told her, while you are looking.

Marija stayed with us for several weeks, occupying one room. Several weeks, was it not longer? They were peaceful weeks. So surprising. As though she had always stayed there, eating, sleeping, getting up there, being together with us. In the afternoons we ate dinner in the dining room, we seldom do that otherwise, we set the table with enthusiasm and took ages discussing places we had visited and foodstuffs we preferred, vacation destinations we would like to revisit. Marija said we must come to Latvia. We must visit her hometown someday, she would show us around. I think we envisioned at that particular time, we would travel with Marija, eat local food, meet the uncle, daughter, grandchild again. The rest of the family.

Both Simon and I participated in these conversations with unusual eagerness.

In the evenings we formed a little group distributed among the settee and our three chairs, never facing the television, but each with a book or bent over the chessboard. Simon showed her his books, the history books with detailed descriptions of areas where important battles have been fought, he had marked all of them on various maps, look at the mountain ranges, these long river courses, I will show you what happened, if you see that line there, what it indicates, he talked as though he himself had seen armies fall on the battlefield. She seemed like a friend, he said later. A true friend, did she not?

She was indeed, I said. That was after she had left, after her dismissal.

They were lovely, those days she stayed here. We have never had many friends.

The new cleaner arrives around ten. Once a week, mostly on Wednesdays. This one works in several other places, before holidays she brings a friend with her, they work together and clean the entire house. I hear the key in the door, and sometimes, if I am not particularly observant or have forgotten that she is coming, I think for a moment that it is Marija out in the hallway. She always calls out her name. It is Ana, she says, or is it pronounced Anna. Then she places the key on the bureau with a little bang. But she doesn't come into the living room to chat, only if there is something in particular. As a rule she gives me instructions before she leaves. She fetches the vacuum cleaner that Marija was in the habit of using. She has pointed out that it needs a new nozzle, really we need a whole new machine, it does not work the way it should, she says.

But she does not insist.

She lets herself out.

And then it is silent again.

IT BECAME SILENT after Marija. She might just as well have let the house remain empty. Removed the furniture in every single room and just left the marks behind, shadows and pale spaces.

It was on my birthday that it began. What I still don't completely understand, and have spent a great deal of time considering. Immediately after that evening I could still blame it on hidden misunderstandings, other interpretations. But now that is of course no longer any consolation, Marija herself helped me to clarify it. For a time it upset me that I could not replay our conversation like a recording in my memory, what was said that evening. All I remember is some disconnected fragments of a conversation. Simon had booked tickets for a concert, a concert by a well-known philharmonic orchestra, several weeks in advance he came and said: What about inviting her to come with us.

Marija? I said, I was taken aback, even though this was actually something we had briefly discussed, that she should celebrate with us.

Why not, he said.

No, I responded, happy, why not indeed. We were in such

agreement, he was fulfilling something I myself had mulled over in my mind. It was his idea. But it could have been mine, if he hadn't managed to come up with it first. She had also talked about the concert in the Grieg Hall, part of the music festival. I wouldn't believe for a moment that she had any ulterior motives about it, she was not trying to persuade me to invite her along, she was not the kind of person who had ulterior motives, I am sure of that. She simply liked to talk about the event, the actual concert, that particular orchestra, I know she also said that we ought to attend, Simon and I, that it was something we shouldn't miss.

I phoned the box office and made reservations. When I first received the tickets, it was as though this had been the intention all along. We always agreed about her, about Marija. That was perhaps why it felt shameful later. Shame that we had been so mistaken about her? In a way it felt like our responsibility. And simultaneously: shame about what we had not spoken about and that had turned into a lie, nothing that could be explained. We participated in it as though it were our own downfall. That was how we saw it.

AT FIRST SHE would not accept the ticket, no, it was impossible. She couldn't. And I recall that birthday, from the morning onward: Outside there is fog, but Simon says that it is going to be fine, that they have said it is going to be a fine day. I hear him out in the kitchen. He is making coffee, he is placing slices of cake neatly on a plate with a napkin.

Happy birthday, he says as he sits down on the edge of the bed.

How old am I, I say.

He just smiles. Kisses me.

The phone rings, once, then once more. I talk to the children. I put down the receiver and look in the mirror. Marija knocks on the door.

It's your birthday, she says. You are going to a concert. Now you'll both have a nice day.

Then you must come too, Simon says.

SHE JUST LAUGHED. But he insisted. When it dawned on her that he was serious, that we really had bought her a ticket, she became solemn and concerned. It was too much, she said, far too much.

Not until we were in the taxi that evening did she become animated again. She had dressed so beautifully, had borrowed a dress from a friend, a short black jacket, with a lilac coat. Stockings with threads like a fine net. She talked to the taxi driver and told him we were going to a concert, as though everybody had to know about this special occasion, she laughed at something he said, her dress, her hairstyle and the stockings obviously made her extra outgoing. I believe the same applied to our silence, her sociability made us slightly self-conscious, and I think she noticed that, because afterward she said something about just being so happy about this, that we were able to go together.

The taxi drew to a halt outside the Grieg Hall. Marija chattered all the way in. When we sat down she talked about what good seats we had, and for the next few minutes she spoke about how long it would be until the concert started. When the conductor made his entrance, she took my hand and squeezed it.

During the first movement, I was aware that we were leaning back, both of us. I breathed in time to the music, she kept hold of my hand. Simon on the other side of me, it was so long since we had been to a concert.

At the intermission she was enthusiastic, we were all enthusiastic.

She was absorbed by the musicians, the conductor, we had bought the program, and Marija peeked inside it on the way out to the lobby. While we were standing there, a couple of Simon's old colleagues walked by, they stopped and expressed surprise at seeing us, and I introduced them to Marija. My friend, I said. They said hello to her.

When we returned to our seats, there were still a few minutes left of the intermission.

She was reading the program, it said something about the conductor.

He is Jewish, she said. She said something further. Something I did not catch, just a single sentence as she turned her head away. No, he isn't, or: Really he can't be. It was trivial. It was a triviality. I thought it over, and let it go.

For the remainder of the concert I forgot everything except the music. It is one of the best concerts I've ever attended, Simon commented afterward. All three of us agreed.

On the way home in the taxi she tried to persuade us that we should hear them again on another occasion. She took my hand again in the backseat, squeezing it tight. I remember that. Thanks, she said. Thanks again.

I PEER OVER at the neighboring garden, the curtains are closed in what I believe has been turned into a utility room. The neighbor has allowed a hedge to grow, he seems preoccupied by his garden. The hedge is not so tall yet, but tall enough, he bought large bushes that he planted and so changed the landscape overnight. Why does that upset me? I must have become fond of continuity, but what does that mean. When there is something you cannot do without, there is a need, it is often called love. I wonder whether he ever invites the girl for a coffee or a mineral water, the young girl who cleans for him, whether they converse.

I have a photograph of Marija. In the photo she is on an outing with us. She is so cheerful, we are having a picnic on a sloping bank in the forest, we are laughing at the picture being taken. It strikes me when I look at it now. Marija in the photograph: She has not said anything yet. She is as she was, before. The picture seems so innocent, she is sitting there. Cheerful, waving, with a lunch box and a thermos flask on her lap.

It feels as though I could have stopped her, intervened on this day that looks so flawless and simple in the picture, held her there, said something or made a move to ward off the action that causes her to leave, to be gone. That she is soon out of our lives.

As though that would have helped anything.

THE PERSON I have been closest to, apart from my children, is Simon. I miss a voice, that is what I miss. Sometimes I miss the time Marija was here so strongly that I cannot comprehend that she has left. I wake and Simon is still by my side. Simon's body, the same long fingers, the same familiar movements when he turns around, sits up in the bed. But he has traveled into himself. The territory we shared is closed off, locked in the same way that I am shut off from Marija. I tell myself that they both exist somewhere. I just have to accept the distance. As it applies to her we are talking about tens of miles, about hours, a day's journey. Perhaps I could have done that someday, journeyed.

I am not going to do it. There is something paradoxical about it, if she had been silent, she would still have been here. But he is the one who is silent, who has gone, without words he becomes almost invisible.

At the beginning, a few letters arrived. Her handwriting, postmarked Latvia on a pale stamp. A pretty little bundle of three or four letters, I don't know what they contain, and I don't know whether more will come, I won't open them anyway. It is done now, I cannot undo it. I saw on television that there was a news report about Latvia, I tried to turn up the volume on the TV. The remote control is faulty and before I managed to do anything, they had changed the topic.

Her words, her voice that day, how she comes into sight, most of the time I am able to shut it out, there is something about the clock, that harsh ticking. When I first hear it, it is more strident than anything else. That is all I hear.

IT WAS SEVERAL months after the concert. We were sitting in the kitchen. Marija was looking through the mail. That morning our neighbor had begun to tidy the lawn with edging shears, the neighbor who sometimes irritates me, the guy who employs the young women. Now he was standing beside the fence busy with this machine, as though he were testing the motor. What is he up to, Marija said, she started to talk about this neighbor. She had mentioned him several times before, or perhaps we had talked together about him. Maybe I was the origin of her displeasure, she may have adopted my antipathy.

We watched him through the kitchen window. Walking along the outer edge of the lawn, holding the machine, stopping it, bending over and clearing something away before starting it up again.

She said it in Latvian. And nevertheless I understood what she said. The tone of voice. The word.

He must be a Jew.

What did you say? I asked.

And she repeated it. So that I should understand.

She stood in the middle of the kitchen, between the table and the window, she was still clutching the bundle of mail, and repeated what she had said. Repeated it calmly in my own language, that he was probably one of them. She said that. *Them.* To be sure that I caught her meaning, she probably wanted to explain.

And then it started. She went on and on, talked and talked. I kept my eyes on the water faucet, the sink, the floor, the window ledge. In the background was the noise of those snarling shears, on and off, on and off. What she said was so banal, like a child retelling a fairy story and rattling off the words of others, stylized and concise, it became an overstated soliloquy in which each word leads on to the next, everything has to be memorized in the right order, because that order is the only logic to be found in the story. It is found only within its own compulsory neurotic framework, its own tautology. Spiteful and simple. The simplicity of the cliché, overused words, the language of tired phrases. About *them.*

I thought she would never finish. When she stopped, it was because of a detail. She had discovered something when she looked at the stack of mail and lifted the letter sitting on top, she asked if this wasn't a letter I had been waiting for. Simon had also come in, I did not know how much of the tirade he had caught, but I could see on his face, the astonishment, that he had heard enough to understand.

She stood with this letter in her hand, as though it really meant something, I must have asked her to open it, for she started to talk about its contents. She was preoccupied by the letter now, she had shifted her focus and was indignant about something she read there.

I sat down on the chair because I had just stood up as though to stop what was going on, as though it could be warded off by such a movement, but of course it couldn't, and when I realized that, at the same time as I realized what it was that had happened, I let myself drop, without resistance down on the chair and it felt like a blow when the seat hit my bottom.

Like a punishment.

WE LOOKED AT each other, Simon and I, that day in the kitchen. He in the doorway, immediately afterward he excused himself and went out. He was going on an errand and was away for several hours, Marija washed the floors upstairs and sorted through some old towels that she was going to throw out. She left early. When he returned, we prepared dinner, he and I, in silence, or a stillness that seemed to contain an enduring intensity, with a low-frequency sound, like a repetition, an echo of the neighbor's machine, the machine that had been on the go all afternoon. We both attempted to ignore it, the alarm, dreadful, low, but just as urgent, insistent. In the evening we read, in our individual chairs in the living room. We postponed it. When we began to talk again, it was only a possibility. By conversing we would reach into that room, I thought, where everything existed, who we were. Who we could not be. What we had tried to avoid.

What we must do. We postponed it, we spent a few days in that condition.

But it turned out exactly like that. That was exactly what happened.

One afternoon he had sat in the chair where he likes to sit. His voice was softer than usual, he was probably trying to keep calm.

We must, he began. It seemed as though he was searching, for an opening in something that was shut tight.

I said: We ought perhaps to try to.

No, he said.

No, I suppose not, I said.

I can't see that it will change anything.

We ought to say, I said, we ought to say something to her.

But what do you think we should say.

We let her go, as Simon put it. She ought to have a reference, I thought. I know how some people treat cleaners. I said that we ought perhaps to give her a reference. But how would that reference look, he said. We arrived at the decision that it would be difficult to write anything supplementary.

Neither of us said anything. To her. And we never told them about it. I did not tell my daughters about what happened, her opinions, her hatred. About Marija. I did not let them in.

I must say something. It can't be kept quiet any longer. But what can I say.

Now it is silent when the cleaner has gone. Silent in the morning and in the evening. We each sit in our individual chairs, he pretends to read, and closes his eyes. I pretend not to notice.

THE MORE I thought about it, the more convinced I became that it was unsuccessful, even that was unsuccessful. The retreat into silence. I should have said something. How could I trust the words so little. Trust my words so little that I had to make her silent. We who talked together, she and I.

But now, when I think about her litany on the kitchen floor, her rendition of the fairy tale. How she makes a speech, she mustn't be interrupted, because then it is possible it will all fall apart. And when she is finished, she will not listen to protests, as there are no arguments that can be used outside this context, it is similar to a religion, it is a system built up in order to nourish itself.

There is no doubt in it.

Her confident speech. And my own voice in the following days, my own and Simon's voice, the search for the words. It is beautiful, I think, doubt.

I REMEMBER ONE more thing about her. I remember that she came, as she had come that first day, that she stood beside the bookcase in the living room, I tried to pretend that everything was as normal, that it was not unpleasant to stand there together. She prattled again, this time about details, practical details, as though she wanted to talk her way through a brick wall, using her speech as a battering ram. I felt everything she said, felt it as though it were me she was trying to penetrate, her explanations about everyday matters, as though she was only taking a vacation and wanted to warn us about practical things we needed to remember while she was gone. Things we must take care of. She said that we must remember to turn the alarm on when we went out, and at night. It is important, she said.

She was really going to travel. She talked about wanting to go back now, that she would go home for a while. To Latvia.

I did not reply. Or I said: That's fine. Have a good trip.

Can I give you a hug? she said. She was gripping the shoulder strap of her bag, a worn strap, she always used that old bag. Her hand clutching the leather strap tightly, stroking it.

Before I managed to say anything, the doorbell rang. A friend came to collect her, they were going on a job together. Once she had stepped through the door, across to the car, she turned and looked back at us. Simon had gone inside, but I was still standing there. The friend said something to Marija. Perhaps that she should sit inside, that they had to drive off. We looked at each other. Did I hesitate just then? I believe I hesitated. But I did not know what I should do, I could not think of a single word that would help. I shut the door.

Marija. I think about it being her birthday, she had her birthday around this time. I have tried to imagine where she is living now, what it looks like there, an apartment in the capital city, her uncle, her daughter, other relatives who have arrived to celebrate her special day. The girl who grinds her teeth and clenches her fists. I cannot write to her.

In the bathroom I see my face in the mirror, the corners of my mouth turned down. Have they always done that, or have they become like that with the passing of time, I think it was something that happened gradually. The mentolabial furrow is the name of the groove that marks the beginning of the chin, it has become deeper while the chin itself seems diminished. I have never liked using makeup. I take out a mascara brush. The sticky consistency on the eyelashes. Lipstick tastes of stearin. A magpie is busy in the garden.

I remember calling out to him. Awhile ago I arrived home after being out shopping. He did not answer. Simon, I called as I walked into the living room, the bedroom, the kitchen. I searched the entire house first, that was when I started to become afraid. It comes creeping, not abruptly, that fear. I went down into the basement, what would he be doing there. I searched the garden.

In the end I rang our neighbor's doorbell, but he was not at home.

I walked across the road, down by the lake. The anxiety growing, I ran home again, I had forgotten the garage, I switched on the light and thought I might perhaps find him there among the skis, the old chairs. I don't know why I thought that, perhaps it was simply the fear. It was empty. When I returned I remained standing by the telephone, before thinking of something. I had seen him go down the garden earlier that day. I shouted again as I ran, and when I pulled back the branches at the foot of the grove of trees, he was sitting on the stump of a blasted tree. Where I found Kirsten sitting many years ago. The stump we had never removed because the children used to balance on it. I never liked them playing down there, hidden behind the trees.

I was scared, I said as I sat down beside him. I was searching for you.

He nodded, uttering not a word, and he did not look at me. But for the first time in ages, he nodded.

•

THE INTRUDER, I recall him as immature and young now that I am older myself. I believe I saw him again at a bus stop many years ago. I was intending to take the bus not far from here. There had been a lot of rain that spring, fine drizzle that washed away the last remnants of winter on the streets and the roads. Is that not the way winter disappears every year, I am never able to notice it, in this city everything is rained away and that's how it has been here for as long as I can remember, the rain that competes only with the fog and the wind, it comes from the front, at an angle, lashing you in the face even if you hold an umbrella before you like a shield, rain in fine vertical lines suspended in the air, or invisible, so light that you don't actually believe it's raining until you arrive home and discover that everything is damp. He was waiting at the bus stop, the one located next to an old tram-way kiosk. I positioned myself at a distance, sheltering from the rain, we were the only ones there, we were waiting for the same bus. He was a few years older now, his hair was hanging down across his forehead, it seemed darker, but that was perhaps because it was wet. It was probably also because of the cold rain that he had a twitch at his mouth, a slight twitch, it could have been conscious or involuntary, he had this twitch, as though the rain was bothering him, but like the dog so many years earlier, he could not drag himself away, could not protect himself, but had to stand there becoming gradually wetter with the rain running down his face, his clothes, his shoes. He looked over at me, a brief glance with no sign of recognition, but I had an urge to say hello. I wanted to greet him, I became confused about this need to demonstrate that I recognized him. At that moment I remembered it differently, that morning he had stood inside my house. I saw before me the undeveloped boyish face, the seriousness in his eyes, the worn-out overcoat he had been wearing, other details popped up, even the hand that accepted the money was transformed in my memory, did it not tremble? And what I had later read in the newspaper, the description of him as confused, I remembered that he had stood there, by my side, facing the children, in the bright open living room with the windows overlooking the terrace and the garden, I thought I had never got to know what he wanted, for me he had simply been an intruder, a threat, but now I thought that he could just as well have been someone seeking refuge. Or searching, for something or someone.

At three o'clock I drive to collect Simon, I drive the usual route, parking in front of the low building with benches outside. And there he is. It is always astonishing that he has managed, that he has got through the day and emerged at the other side. Sometimes he smiles and seems almost secretive. Other times he is exhausted and falls asleep in the car on the way home.

If I go inside, I find him in the room with the people in whose company he spends the day. A young caregiver who is always there, I cannot hear his voice, but through the glass door I can see that he is talking to Simon, at one point he kneels down, and his white trouser legs are stretched at the knees as he explains something and Simon looks at what he is showing him.

Simon himself is sitting between two women as if between two soft rocks, one with hair like white foam, he seems to participate with pleasure in the making of a rug, but they are obviously talking above his head. I see their mouths moving as they work. Or is it two parallel monologues, I can't know that of course, I can't hear through the door. I look at his hands. The hands I loved to feel on my spine, my breasts. The same hands that examined patients, comforted our children.

A skinny woman, one of the patients, suddenly begins to clap, and the similarity to an assembly at kindergarten is striking. At the same time I see that Simon is involved, it seems as though he considers it is not too bad.

He looks at me as I come in, they all look at me, as though I am intruding. He makes a grimace. Of happiness or displeasure? Or does he see my embarrassment, and is making fun of me? *You always worry too much.*

They call out their goodbyes, see you tomorrow. He smiles.

I STOP OFF at a few stores on the way home. He is clearly content to accompany me on the shopping trip, as though I have devised something for his entertainment. We have now developed the habit of him waiting in the car, I'll be back soon, I say and he nods. But today I open the door at his side and wait for him to stand on his feet, we walk between the aisles and both of us pick up items, as we have always done. He still walks slightly too fast, I have to call to him to wait. Why do you take so long, he used to say, we have a list with us you know, the food will be out of date before we get home. His teasing. You're always running a marathon, I said, there's nobody here giving out medals. He liked that I answered back. Now he gathers apples into a bag, weighing them on the scale hanging above the counter. He enjoyed charming the girls at the checkout, cracking jokes. They knew him in this supermarket, before. Now there's a new girl here, someone who works part time, I usually say hello to her, she doesn't have that bored expression most of the other checkout operators adopt, we chat a little, once I almost asked her if she ever tired of her job. Fortunately I didn't say that. Simon wants to help me with the bags as we are packing them into the car, he lifts them up, one by one. It strikes me that he is trying to demonstrate his presence. And then we are home again. After dinner I have the feeling that he is watching me as I load the dishwasher, but when I turn around he has already left the room.

When I walked past the church in late summer last year, I saw that the plastic sheeting placed over the façade was being tugged aloft by the wind, it was standing proud like a flag and then falling back. Until being lifted again a few seconds later. I liked to walk past even when there were no others there. Occasionally I saw the pastor. He might be standing outside on the gravel talking to a couple of the workmen, once he was standing in front of his car.

I stopped to say hello to him, and he was keen to show me how the work was progressing, they were happy with what had been done, he said. He told me a little about the church building. The architect who had designed it in the thirties. We chatted for a while. He asked how Simon was getting on.

And before I answered, he said that becoming old isn't easy, not for any of us. When he said that, he cast his eyes down, as though he were ashamed of complaining. I often walked past the church during the fall months. The air was clear and fresh, it was no longer warm. The improvements had been going on for a while by then, I wondered when it would become visible, whether the change would be something you would notice.

I DID NOT see him again until December. It was cold then. I had intended to walk around the lake, it was a normal weekday, in the morning. I had not expected to meet anyone, but walked there concentrating on keeping my coat closed, as a button had fallen off when I was putting it on, and I had let it be, because I had not wanted to miss the walk. There was something about the cold weather, the frost on the bare trees and ice on the water. I saw at once that it was him, he was wearing a big gray jacket, like a member of an Arctic expedition, perhaps that was what made him look leaner. Or else he had lost weight during the course of the weeks I had not seen him. He stood peering at the water, like the boy I used to see down there. I followed his gaze the short distance to the edge of the lake, where the dirt had solidified and the frost had settled, and toward the white expanse covering the water, surprisingly intact, even though the more fragile layer at the edge indicated that it was not safe.

I said hello as I approached. He looked at me more in confusion than surprise.

Hello, he said.

We walked together for a short distance. Perhaps he had been ill, I thought. He was not so young, he had said himself of course that getting old was not easy. I thought he seemed worn out, but I could not ask if there was anything more. We strolled around to the other side, it seemed as though a line had been drawn across the ice at the southern end of the lake, a trail as if someone had walked there. He stopped to examine his winter shoes, one of the laces was slack, I looked away as he bent down to tie it, glancing out at the expanse of ice, the extremities that lay there, as though they were frozen solid. I regretted talking to him, I wanted to go. But then he stood up again, and we continued, on our way around the lake.

He said that when he was a child, some teenagers almost drowned in the water here. There was a huge rescue operation, and the youngsters were kept back by the adults. He recalled how he himself had raced down to have a look together with a crowd of other children and were held back.

There were people trying to crawl out to the water channel, he said, and they got the teenagers out in the end.

I glanced at him. As he spoke he was staring at the water, the ice.

My brother was one of them, he said.

I nodded.

He said he had always wondered what had caused them to go out onto the unsafe ice. Whether it was a feeling of invincibility or inertia that made some people try that kind of thing.

They were only young, of course, I said. He said yes, that I was right there.

I looked fleetingly at him. I thought he might say that something like that could cause one to doubt, but he did not say that. Besides it had ended well.

I'm so happy to be here, he said. But it gives me a guilty conscience.

I was uncertain whether he meant the place by the lake, where we were standing at that moment, or the church or simply existence in general.

He spoke softly, not like when he was preaching, when he was standing in the church. But it could have been part of a sermon. I waited for the rest of it, but he said nothing more.

He kicked a lump of ice over the hardened dirt, toward the surface of the lake.

Ice on water, he said. Otherwise it always seems to be raining here.

It will start again soon, I said.

Do you think so, he said and laughed. We both laughed.

We went back the same way.

And when I looked at him, I wanted to raise my hand and stroke his temple. I imagined doing that. What he would have said, his astonishment.

ONCE DURING THE course of that winter I went into the church and sat down, the door was open. I looked again at the altarpiece and the baptismal font. The space inside the church seemed brighter. The pews in front of me were empty, it was just as silent as the first time I had seen the pastor there.

After a while someone came and sat down at the far end of the same pew, when I turned around, it was the pastor. We sat there for a while without speaking, like the day he had walked with me and we had stopped for a second and looked at the water. Of course I didn't know much about him, but when I saw him with people from the congregation, I gained the impression that he was well liked. Perhaps they were the ones he had, they were the ones he was attached to.

I thought now that the works were finished, he would not be there so often, he would not stand outside talking to the workers, following the work, they too would soon be finished with what they were doing. And the church door would be locked as it had always used to be.

LATER I TALKED to him a couple of times. It dawned on me that perhaps I was searching all the same for a listener in a context such as that. A backdrop, a superstructure that offered an opportunity. An opportunity for something I am unable to articulate. I could not walk by, that was what I felt. It was as if I had postponed something, and now I could not walk by, push it away any longer. The actual building located there, that I often stroll past on my walks, is like an assertion I have tried not to respond to, something I have delayed. I envy individual people their piety, their conviction. Those who have not appreciated the need for belief and consolation, they are truly naïve. Naïve enough to go to bed each night and get up again each morning without giving a thought to the despondency that surrounds them. But the need does not make one into a believer. At least it hasn't done so for me. I would so like to understand. I have been at Sunday school and children's lessons of course, but it is like different dots on a sheet of paper, suggesting the outlines of something, a certain shape, but there is no line drawn between them.

I like the actual story. The writer who is wise and reasonable, intelligible dramatic art, a plain and simple, but not stupid narrative, the narrator has his hidden intentions that will be revealed along the way, the protagonist falls into various traps, but first and foremost in order to learn from it, never so serious that he cannot be saved, and all the threads are drawn together in an inalterable conclusion.

When I recall clergymen from my youth, I remember best the distance, the respect. I have carried two of my daughters before men like them, I assume they really believe that they have had a call from God. As far as the baptism was concerned I did not go through with it because anyone insisted, it was just what one did. Then I held the tiny bare heads above the baptismal font and doubted as the sign of the cross was made from their forehead to their chest and from side to side, and just as much afterward. One of them screaming and sweaty and bundled up in a handed-down scrap of material one uses on that kind of occasion, the other silent and staring at me as if I were about to immerse her in the sea and let her drift down to its sandy bed. Solemn, resigned. The youngest is not baptized.

The interior, the sacristy. A place to go with a feeling of guilt. Perhaps you hand over the feeling of guilt in a church because you do not know what else to do with it. In order to find a place where significance is assigned to it, with no objections raised. There are so few places to go that you can attach significance to, as Marija once said.

The pastor probably thought I was a believer, or had become so in my old age, out of anxiety or regret.

The feeling of guilt. It belongs with that uneasiness, that transitory uneasiness that can surface when I wake during the night and lie there without falling asleep again. Did I want to seek out the church in order to hold that up against a background of deeper meaning? If I wished to be closer to the church. Can't it simply have been a desire to be part of something, a context, or at least some kind of contact? But perhaps it is also partly a feeling of guilt. Guilt, that binds us to others just as much as every other emotion. Perhaps more.

HE WOULD HAVE been so much older now, my son, I have difficulty picturing him in my mind. I kept his clothes, the clothes he did not take with him. They are in the basement. I did not use them for the girls, I must have felt that they were his. Or perhaps it was for my own sake that I did not make use of them for any of the other children.

I went to find him, after all the years and the silent battle between us, Simon and me. Maybe I did it for Simon's sake, but it may also have been for my own. I wanted to see who he had become, what he would say to me, whether I had caused anything, any harm. It was only a couple of years ago. I found the name Simon had kept safe and looked up an address in a newly renovated area. I stood for a while on that street, looking at the entrance to an apartment block where the residents were coming and going, and at one point I spotted a youngish man and two little girls emerge from the stairway at the front of the building, one of the girls had an umbrella under her arm that she was trying to open, her father tried to help her, and after several attempts the child obviously became impatient and rushed inside the entrance, with her father following after. The door slammed behind them. I thought that it could have been him, for a second I thought that, but I knew it did not add up. It wasn't him, he was too young. I hesitated slightly before finding the apartment number I had been given, and finally rang the doorbell. I stood on the sidewalk and glanced up at the façade. There was traffic in the street, cars driving past. A woman leaned out from one of the windows above me, supporting herself with her forearms on the windowsill, taking a couple of puffs of her cigarette, peering down at me, before closing the window again. No one opened the door, I rang the doorbell a few more times. There was no one at home, perhaps I was just there at the wrong time of day.

I took the bus home. I let it lie, I was cowardly and did

not tell Simon about it. I was relieved, but perhaps I was also, without quite being able to explain it, disappointed.

They phoned later from an office that had given me assistance, I had asked them to call. The woman I spoke to on the phone asked whether I had found my way, and when I said I was unsure whether I had been given the correct name and address, replied in a subdued voice that it was possible to continue the search, it sometimes took time, families could for example have moved abroad, and as though she guessed something from my response, a doubt, she added that we would certainly be successful if I really wanted to be.

A PHOTOGRAPH WAS taken of us. Me with the child, my son, before I gave him away. He is leaning back slightly, perhaps he was afraid of the flash, I don't remember who took it. I am sitting ramrod straight with the baby, the infant balanced on my knee as though he can really sit up on his own, but I am supporting him with both hands, otherwise he would obviously fall over, he is unsteady, but I am holding him with the palms of my hands parallel, as though I were holding a parcel, a bag, if you removed the child from the picture, it would just look as though I were measuring something, demonstrating the thickness, the width, there is no pride in my expression, no happiness. I am looking at the back of his head. As he pulls backward. I have no idea where it comes from, whose idea it was to take this despondent photograph. Perhaps it was taken at the adoption office, or earlier that same day. I search my facial expression on that day, and think I discern something, is it guilty conscience, shame?

It is a dream now, remote and hazy. I tend this grave belonging to a stranger. It is always silent in the afternoon, I like to be here, around Christmastime I buy a wreath, there are lanterns placed on some of the graves at that time of year, there are other people going around arranging things. No one asks me who I am here for. Actually I don't know myself either.

It can be called a memory trace in the brain. I read it somewhere. When a memory is first laid down, after enough time has elapsed and it has been recalled enough times, the synaptic alterations can become permanent. And parts of the brain used to retain the memory are not necessary to call it forth, it has become like a trace, a photograph, a picture that is maybe always going to be found there.

Simon was preoccupied by the suitcase. During the years he was searching for his cousin and aunt, trying to find traces of them, he continually returned to the suitcase, his aunt's suitcase that he remembered from the apartment before they had to leave for the hiding place. He wondered whether others might be able to help, whether it might be possible to track it down. His aunt's suitcase that she had packed because she was waiting for her husband to fetch her, they would go into hiding together. He had seen it with his own eyes, it was a suitcase of the type that was common at that time, with mountings at the corners, canvas and leather material, straps to stretch over the clothes to keep them in place. He cannot remember his cousin's face, but he remembers the suitcase clearly. It sat in the hallway, a suitcase like the ones belonging to his parents that later, after the war were always placed in an attic, and never taken out again because they do not travel, the two elderly people have become unschooled in everything to do with transport, they shut themselves increasingly inside the apartment. The suitcases were purchased in the same place, both those of his parents and his aunt's. He has seen her opening it, taking things out and snapping the locks closed again, he imagines that it contained clothes, towels, toothbrushes and washcloths. His parents were also fed up with his aunt's suitcase, they thought it was in the way, it was both optimism and obstinacy, they said, that made her refuse to unpack. Nevertheless they accepted it, bore with it, and with her plans. She was sorry she was unable to go into hiding with them, but insisted that her husband would collect her. She was young, they said when they talked about it, young and afraid.

He believes that on the day they were taken away, she had the suitcase with her, although it is not likely, a suitcase is overstating things, it has no place in all this. All the same, he imagines the suitcase. That she somehow or other manages to take it with her, that it accompanies her. She and her son, they sleep beside it, perhaps they even sit on it if there is room to do that. (Actually he knows that there is no room either to sleep or for a suitcase), they stay close beside it all the time, it would be a simple matter for someone to steal it or its contents, they must only hope. She always used to talk about what she had packed, his aunt, because it was important. Something materializes through the suitcase and its contents, a kind of tidiness and security. The suitcase and its contents bear witness to a possible destination for the journey, where things will be unpacked and put in their place. The clothes will be worn, the bedclothes will be slept in. The suitcase is a guarantee that this is actually a journey like other journeys, with the definition of such transportation always incorporating the possibility of traveling back to where you started. But at the terminus, where they are expelled, wrenched from the train together with all the others, it is taken from her. The suitcase is flung onto a pile of other people's luggage. Then she stands there, Simon says. Without the suitcase. Is her son standing by her side? At that moment it dawns on her that they are not going to travel any farther.

HE HAS RECOUNTED this, and I have visualized it. It is easy to envisage those two. In a crowd of people, I think. In a herd being thrust backward and forward in a confined space, the two of them also jolted to and fro, caught among the others, dragged in one direction and then another, and at one moment during this scene, I imagine that they are separated, mother and son. Lose sight of each other. Those two who have been so close during these months alone in the apartment.

In everything that happens, in this movement of people who are shouting, falling, remnants of luggage, bundles being trampled, coats and winter jackets, infants and old people, his cousin is left standing on his own. He turns around, but sees no faces, only vague impressions, shapes, apparitions, hears complaints, shouts, sobbing from children like himself. Around him grows this mountain of people in motion, like a wall, a terrible, unstable wall from which parts are ripped away while new ones are added. Is he wearing something, something that gives him sufficient weight to remain standing on exactly that spot without being jostled along or knocked over? Perhaps a narrow rucksack or some other possession he is carrying, something he is now probably holding with both hands, clutching it to his chest. As though he is embracing it, keeping it safe and clinging to it at the same time. While the human wall continues to be shoved backward and forward once more, and simultaneously increases, like an organism through mitosis, a cell division before his very eyes. The boy's mother is still part of this formation, and is carried forward like a light object being propelled onward by the current in a river. But the boy, the cousin, remains standing on the same spot. While he waits, he cannot do anything else of course, for her to be carried back to him.

In the evening we watch TV. Simon sits in his chair. I am uncertain whether he follows the action, although sometimes he too switches on the set, perhaps one of the things he does automatically, from old habit. There is something paradoxical about his benevolence toward this screen, with all its pestering, jabbering that never ends, even when there is the occasional break, it demands attention. He stares at the screen regardless of what is being shown, as though it is exactly that and nothing else he has been waiting for. I ask if it's a bit cold, whether I should fetch a jacket. In the wardrobe I catch sight of the snail shell still lying there, I hold it in my hand for a moment. It is solid, but when I hold it up to the lamp, the light shines through the delicate edges. I wonder when the snail disappeared, why it abandoned such a perfect place, the exquisite curved corridor. I stroke the surface, a golden veneer, brittle and yet durable, before replacing it and closing the door.

I put the jacket over Simon's shoulders, he nods as though I have asked him something. Perhaps it is a delayed reply. The TV continues droning. I open the book that Helena has left on the coffee table, the book about the First World War, I look quickly through it. Here is the old Europe. Lost platoons of soldiers, trench warfare on the western front. Attempts to break through. The Battle of the Somme. For days, months the slaughter continues, from July to November, the young boys fall through the paper pages. Names such as Tannenberg, Somme, Verdun. Between the dust jacket and the first page there is a folded sheet of paper. *To my girls* it says on this folded sheet. He has written it in his slightly shaky handwriting. Of course I don't know how long it has lain there, but it is Simon's handwriting, it must have been written more than a year ago, while he was still able to write.

I feel helpless at the sight of this letter that I had not asked to see. As with the application form, I don't know what I should do with it. I stand there hesitating, before opening it and reading.

Not so long ago, when I was looking through some of our old papers, the papers belonging to Simon and me, I found another letter, or a rough draft of something that was probably intended to be a letter. I recognized the handwriting, it was inside a blank envelope, but I was unsure whether it was of any significance, it took some time for me to realize what it contained. When Simon was a relatively newly qualified physician, he made a friend. A friendship he later maintained through all these years. They went out and had dinner with other colleagues, and I think they talked about their work since they were in the same profession. It was a formal friendship, I don't imagine that they ever confided much, a conventional relationship, deriving from and dependent on the codes that applied to friendship at that time. Naturally it came about that we invited this friend and his wife to various social events. We used to send them Christmas cards, in fact it was often me who wrote them. The couple responded with postcards to us every Christmas, formally decorated cards with the obligatory greetings.

I had never considered the friendship to be close enough to include letters, on the contrary. A personal letter seemed to conflict with the distance and formality that the limited seasonal contact depended upon. The letter must also have been an attempt to break through the conformity. Simon wrote to this man, his wife had evidently been ill, I couldn't remember anything about it. He tried to comfort him and say something beyond their well-established politeness. He had obviously given up the effort since the letter had never been sent. It was so helpless, what was stated on the sheet of paper, there were several forms of words embarked upon, crossed out, as though he had tried to arrive at a sentence or a collection of them that could cover something he perhaps did not even grasp himself. Or perhaps he had some idea, but these sentences and attempts were far too much of a contrast to what their friendship had been up to that point. In order to achieve that, he had to go beyond the boundaries of what was possible, who he himself could and would appear to be, and so he became all the more constrained by his own limits. It seemed so desperate.

I felt sorry for him, and all the same I was annoyed that I had been kept outside, that he had not mentioned anything to me.

I THINK ABOUT this letter to his colleague now that I am reading what he has attempted to write to his daughters. For the letter is to them. I can see that he has tried, he has really tried to formulate something, and if they had opened it, they would have seen his handwriting and these attempts to describe, impart, pass something on, to them. To Helena and her sisters. But he cannot. He has to give up, it is a long time since he was clever at that. It is only a rough draft, a sheet of paper he has left there all the same. *Dear Helena, Greta and Kirsten*, he writes, *I have something I—* He gives up. A fresh attempt. He is sorry that it has taken so long, he is sorry about it all. He writes that he first bought paper for a letter, that the storekeeper misunderstood, he got the wrong kind. *Today the first signs of summer are here,* he writes, *the summer is going to be fine, I do think so. And I hope that you all manage to have a vacation. Mother and I both consider that you work too hard. But I have always worked too hard myself, so it is obviously hereditary, that kind of thing. Now I have decided to tell you something I have neglected to say for far too—*

I can't manage to interpret the continuation of the sentence, it is nearly rubbed out because of a faulty pen. But I believe the final word is *long*. Far too long. *My girls,* he continues, *you have become so big. So grown up.* He starts over again, trying to find an introduction.

I become angry, I become angry because he has decided to tell them on his own, without having talked to me about it first.

He is still sitting with his gaze directed at the screen. I don't feel sorry for you, I want to say. You sit there and are immune. No matter what I say, you are going to stare into space and smile. I want to face him. Listen, Simon, don't turn away. I don't feel sorry for you. You let me down, I want to say.

How could he let me down like this, leave me behind in silence with this letter? I want to tell him.

He just sits there.

What can I say?

There he sits. In his chair, and there is nothing to say.

I sit on the settee beside the chair, placing my fingers on

his lips. I love you, I think. Have I said it, I can't recall whether I have said it, but I really must have. I remember that I tried to purge the word from my pupils' vocabulary, because they loved everything and nothing, eradicating all meaning. It is a word that doesn't say anything, I told them.

Simon looks at me. In the background a woman is waving from the TV screen, she is standing on the deck of a boat gliding across the water. His name, I think. Simon. It means someone who listens.

DARKNESS HAS FALLEN by the time I fetch the telephone and dial the number. It rings for a long time. The sleepy voice. I have awakened her.

Mom, Helena's voice says, why are you phoning now?

Was it you who placed the letter in the book, I think. I am about to say it. But I don't say it. I know she hasn't read it, none of them has read it.

I have a lot of old photographs, I say. Perhaps you could help me to sort them out? They take up too much space, old trash. Photographs and letters.

Letters? She says. Is everything all right, with you and Dad?

I see my reflection in the glass door, outside there is the dark garden, the garden furniture that I have put out on the terrace, the chairs leaning forward on the table. The waxed tablecloth folded up. Soon we'll put them in the shed, when the summer is over.

Her voice again. Are you there? she asks.

Yes, I say.

She waits, we both wait.

Mom, says Helena, was there something else you wanted to say?

One time in winter I found him at the bus stop right over here. Everywhere was completely white, there were several days with an unusual amount of snow for Western Norway. He must have put on his overcoat, the boots that I ought to have hidden, but that I didn't dare put away because I was scared he would go out all the same, in his socks. Those continual outings of his. I noticed after an hour that he was gone, I looked in all the places I always do when I can't find him, in the garage, in the grove of trees, I thought about driving up to the church. I took the car that had become covered in snow overnight, I had to shovel the snow and scrape the frost from the windshield. When I was driving along the road, I spotted him, he was sitting on a bench and I think he had closed his eyes, I became so furious, I thought how can he shut his eyes now, how can he just sit there with his eyes closed. I steered the car in to the curb and stopped slightly too abruptly, perhaps he was surprised at someone stopping, I got out of the car, sat down beside him, I said that he could try for my sake, to stay in one place. That sad expression of his. He opened his mouth first of all, but then closed it, and I did not even know whether he intended to say something or was only yawning. I clearly recall the next thing that happened: As I am about to say that we must go home now, I see that he has leaned forward, he raises his hand, I don't know whether he is pointing or simply holding it aloft. In front of us on the asphalt the snow from the snowdrifts along the road is whipped up by the wind, forming waves that are wiped away and then reshaped, downward and downward, fresh waves all the time, the movement seems so gentle, accidental, but nevertheless creating the same pattern all the time, and I look at him, and I feel a powerful desire for him to look back at me, but he stares straight ahead, captivated by the movement, what the wind is doing with the snow, and this is his choice, I think, to come here and sit in this place, and there is nothing I can question. I remain sitting there with him, watching the same movements, over and over again, of the wind and the snow.

IT IS SO late in the summer now. He still goes off on his own at times. He wakes in the morning and goes out the door. He finds the shoes I have hidden, opens the door I have locked. Perhaps I ought to hide the shoes so well that he cannot find them, or put a new lock on the door. I let him go. He is old, but I think he walks down the road quickly, only at the bottom of the hill does he hesitate. I wonder whether his restlessness makes him walk on or whether he just stands there waiting for me or someone else to find him. If he chooses to take the bus into the city, he is probably alone this early in the morning, perhaps he greets the driver before finding a seat. While the bus drives on, Simon sits at the window and looks out. Sees that the city seems desolate and new, the streets resembling wide, empty canals.

Now I have problems thinking about the rest. When does he alight, does he stay on until the terminus? In any case he once took Fløibanen, the funicular railway, a mechanical hand that hoisted him up along the mountainside, up above the city. Here he is among the tourists and strangers. When he reaches the top, he walks to the viewpoint, where we used to go when the children, our girls, were younger. He surveys down below, observing houses and buildings, the fish market under the mist, under the rain. To people watching him, it might look as though he is searching for something.

Once he ends up at a family's house in the Nøstet area. He knocks on the door. They come out, the people who live there. It is a small, old white house, they are an astonished group who peer out. They have just risen from their beds, and here is a strange man on the stairs, an elderly man. Can they help him with anything? Has he lost his way?

He has a cell phone with my number clearly visible. When I arrive to collect him, they say that he is sitting in the living room. Shamefaced I enter this house, through the hallway in the abode of strangers. He is seated as if at a party, a pleasant visit, but at this impromptu gathering, this party, there is nobody who knows him. They follow us with their eyes, mother, father and two children, the youngsters are still in their pajamas. He sits on the settee with a cat on his lap. He strokes its back and nods to me as though this is something we often do. As though we too belong here.

I TAKE OUT the letter from Simon to Helena, and find the photographs I have made up my mind to show her. Relatives, my own family, and his. The pictures are from before the war, Simon as a child, there is even a class photograph there. His family is standing outside the apartment where he lived when he was growing up. There are several family photographs, special occasions with other relatives assembled, and while I look, I catch sight of someone I have not noticed before. At the foot of one of the old photographs is a boy, a young boy. He is wearing a long shirt that may cause him to be taken for a girl. But it is a boy, I look at the haircut, the stiff kneesocks that cover his legs. He is sitting slightly crouched, and his expression is eradicated by the movement or by what seems to be an erosion, disintegration of the photograph, it is in the process of falling to pieces. I recall photographs I have seen of various missing persons, people who have been lost for some reason or other, who are depicted in newspapers and magazines. And there is only the photograph left, it seems like the most important thing they have left behind. When you look at it, you think that it will explain something in some way or other. But it is only a photograph. I put it together with all the other items I have brought out, some papers, the application form that I have decided not to fill in. We are going to sit here at the table tomorrow, Helena and I, and set out the photographs. I see it in my mind's eye already. The past, all these lives, they make up a mosaic. Like the colored panes of glass in the church when the light shines through and makes the motifs clearer. I think about what we are going to say, what I must say, recount. Whether I find the words for it. Now they lie there, the old photographs and pictures, the detailed letters from Irit Meyer, the letters that stopped arriving long ago.

YESTERDAY I FOUND Simon sitting outside the retail center on a bench. A young girl was sitting by his side. She had a Chinese jump rope in her hands, one of the kind I remember from my childhood, it was evidently broken, and she was trying to join the ends together while she chatted, she dropped the rope on the ground, bent down and picked it up, all the time looking in his direction. It looked as though they were conversing. She was talking, showing him something with her hands, holding them up, trying to tie the ropes, straying from the point of what she was saying. He was clearly listening the entire time, turned toward her. I remained standing. Just standing watching. I had been searching for him for over an hour, I had encountered a neighbor, someone who tapped on the car window and pointed toward the retail center.

He was listening to the girl, it might seem that he was absorbed in what she was telling him. I waited for a while before approaching them. The girl did not look up immediately, she was so preoccupied by what she was saying, it was Simon who turned around and noticed me. He smiled. His hair was tousled, glinting in the sunlight, he was wearing the overcoat he is so fond of, that thin coat. The girl followed his gaze, and when it rested on me, she stopped talking. Waited before asking who I was.

I was about to give my name, but I realized it was not my name she meant. She wanted to know what I was doing there, why I was interrupting them, their conversation. What gave me the right to stand there.

He is my, I commenced in an attempt to explain, and before I got to say *husband*, she said: He is nobody's.

I looked at her as she gathered her ropes in a bundle in her fist.

He can't be anybody's. He isn't a thing.

She stood up, she looked at him in disappointment. At me. She walked across the parking lot and on past a car, behind a sign at the exit somewhere she disappeared.

He was left there, smiling. I was looking for you, I said.

I said that he must not leave me. You mustn't leave me, I said.

Simon smiled. I had an urge to slap him. I had an urge to slap something or someone.

I'm so tired, I said.

He placed his hand on the back of mine, stroking it so rapidly it may be that he simply brushed against it. I looked at my hand, at him.

He smiled, but he looked at me.

WHAT AN IMPRESSIVE church, Marija said one time we went there for a walk, she, Simon and I. She wanted to go inside. It's probably not open, I said. It is beautiful, she said. Look at the doors. We stepped down between the trees, she read the gravestones, read the names aloud, and we sat down on a bench, she had brought coffee, we sat there and drank coffee. She said that every time she saw a church, it cheered her up, she thought about the people inside, that it was one of the few places a person could go and feel something significant. There is so little that is as significant. Did she say that? I don't remember what reply we made. She felt so secure, she said, when she saw a church.

I have considered why I went into the church, it may have been a desire to speak to the pastor. It is possible I had some idea that his faith, or at least his conviction in that context, would reveal itself to me too. Reveal. It was a word I often thought about. But when I walked past the church last year, it was the mundane that came to light more than ever before. I observed the church building, the plaster, a broken toilet that was being removed, windowpanes being replaced. I saw that the repair work on the façade had been completed, there was no more to be done, and the pastor came over and spoke, we were both preoccupied by the building work, the changes. Improvements, as he called them. But I saw it in his eyes, the tiredness after the weeks he had been away. I continued to go to the graveside in the spring. I often thought about asking for a consultation, but why would I go there, why seek him out. Did I believe that something or other would come to light if I talked to him, and that we would discover whether I was really guilty of something. How could he decide that. I wanted him to tell me. Tell me who is buried outside, the young man. What he perhaps said in his eulogy, there must have been something to say, something that was recounted to him or to others. Perhaps about a girlfriend, his mother, there has to be an explanation for why she is not there, why the grave is not tended, perhaps she is old, she hasn't got the energy. He is not alone. The pastor could perhaps have told me about it. I pictured in my mind's eye that I arrived there and sat with him, while we waited for me to find my way to the words for what was causing such pain.

IT WAS BY chance, and certainly not planned, that we talked to each other in the spring, that we had a lengthy conversation in the sacristy.

While I spoke about things that are hazy for me now afterward, he had not moved his position, but kept his arm on the armrest, with his hand supporting his chin and head. His clerical robes were probably hanging in the closet behind him. He sat just as still, concentrating, the sunlight was the only thing in the room that had stirred, it struck the windowsill and slid tentatively toward the table where it was captured in a smallish rectangle.

I attempted to explain something, but I understood that it did not allow itself to be spoken so easily, and I felt rather like Simon probably had when he tried to formulate a letter to his colleague. I said that there are things I haven't told anyone, not even my daughters.

I shifted my gaze out the window, the enormous linden trees out there providing a kind of peace.

No one knows who we are. No one except for me.

He did not reply. It was silent in the room, I missed the banging, the sounds from the workmen outside.

He said something inconsequential, that I mustn't see it like that, that it isn't too late to have a conversation with the people close to you. But I think he understood that it was meaningless, because his voice tailed off. And I thought of what he had told me about the teenagers who were drowning, about the adults who held the children back on the shore while others tried to crawl out, the open channel, the teenagers being dragged under the ice-cold water. His task, I thought as I sat there looking at the pastor, is to give comfort. And, I suppose, to find the goodness in all humanity.

As though goodness is something always waiting to be found.

•

THERE IS ONLY a younger clergyman there now. He says hello when I meet him.

When I walk past the church it does not seem so unfamiliar. The scaffolding that was there for several months is long gone. The building is the same, I still feel the distance when I look at it. Nothing has revealed itself, none of what I had perhaps hoped for, but I liked talking to him, the older pastor. I do not know what kind of meaning it had. Perhaps it was simply our conversation, the little clumsy words. Doubt. The last time I was there we sat in the little room again, he had told me that he was going to leave, that he had obtained employment elsewhere. He was looking forward to going, he said.

He accompanied me out. I still remember that afternoon. Our footsteps were muffled by the floor covering. It felt as though we had taken part in a ceremony. This is the way you walk back to your seat after Holy Communion, down between the pews; outside in the vestibule the door is heavy, like a prison door that opens, and we emerge into the light, it is a warm spring evening with the sun dappling the foliage, and on the other side of the lake I know that people are walking, but there is no one else here, only the two of us. His cell phone emits an angry buzzing noise, but he does not look at it. He takes my hand, we say a couple of things to each other. Have a good journey home, he says as though I have a long trip ahead of me, as I step across the gravel, glancing at all the stones and statues and patches of earth where people have planted in the hope of something more than ashes and bone, something that can give peace to the survivors.

I come to a halt beside the gate and wheel around, he is walking slowly up the stairs, I peer across the field to the road, the entrance to the avenue where the linden trees have cast shadows in the lethargic spring light. I look back at him one more time, but the door is closed and the little church seems empty and forsaken.

A LETTER ARRIVED recently, a brown envelope, a precisely folded sheet of paper, the letter heading with the name of the organization Simon had long kept in contact with. It was a brief letter giving the names of two relatives. K. Mendelburg and A. Mendelburg. Date of birth and date of death in Theresienstadt. I understood that one was the cousin he had been searching for. The letter explained what had happened in short, informative turns of phrase. Nothing to hold on to, no details providing a picture or impression of the events being described, now more than seventy years later.

The same day the letter came, I walked past the church again, and stopped beside the wall, perhaps because those few sentences in the letter had affected me, what they described as well as everything they did not say, and I needed a place to go with that emotion I did not even comprehend, so I also remained standing looking at the grave and the plants from the garden that had rooted so well, it even seemed that they were thriving better in their new setting.

I stood there for a while before starting out on the journey home. But it was not the boy, the cousin who had probably been five or six years old, whom I saw in my mind's eye. It was my son, six months old, in the office that afternoon I gave him away. I don't know what I feel when I think about it. I picture his face immediately before he is carried off, when I was encouraged to say goodbye and give him a hug, that is the way I remember it at least, and he looked at me, the only person he knew in the room. He was wearing a tiny blue and white cap that was first taken off and then put back on again. He looked at me, with a gaze I now recall as older, wiser, with some idea of what was waiting. It is terrifying, it unsettles me. But there is no longer anything I can do. And finally someone came and lifted him up and out of my arms. He glanced back at me one more time. Before they carried him off.

It was only that one moment.

I did not see him again after that.

MERETHE LINDSTRØM has published several collections of short stories, novels, and a children's book. She was nominated for the Nordic Council Literature Prize and the Norwegian Critics' Prize for her short-story collection *The Guests*. In 2008 she received the Dobloug Prize for her entire literary work. *Days in the History of Silence* is her most recent novel, winner of the Nordic Council Literature Prize and the Norwegian Critics' Prize for Literature, and nominated for the P2 Listeners' Novel Prize and the Youth Critics' Prize. She lives in Oslo, Norway.

ANNE BRUCE graduated from Glasgow University with degrees in Norwegian and English and has traveled extensively throughout Scandinavia on lecture and study visits. She has translated Wencke Mühleisen's *I Should Have Lifted You Carefully Over*, Jørn Lier Horst's *Dregs*, and Anne Holt's *Blessed Are Those Who Thirst*.